THE BITS BETWEEN
THE ADVERTS

ISBN 0 947848 10 X

First published 1994
by Caron Publications
Peak Press Building
Eccles Road
Chapel-en-le-Frith
Derbyshire SK12 6RQ

Typeset and printed
in England by
PEAK PRESS LIMITED
Chapel-en-le-Frith
Derbyshire

THE BITS BETWEEN THE ADVERTS

by

BARRY HILL

For Avril - above all, my best friend

caron
PUBLICATIONS

Chapel-en-le-Frith

Cover and illustrations by Peter Caldwell

FOREWORD

GREYBRIDGE Central Station was deserted as I made my way wearily down the steps to Platform Three. It had been a long day, and the portable typewriter and briefcase I was carrying became heavier at every step. It wasn't the most pleasant place on earth to be at eight o'clock on a Tuesday evening as the icy jaws of winter began to tighten their grip.

Yet looking down on the town from my elevated vantage point, the myriad of lights glinting and glistening, beacons of hope in a dank, cold world, I felt nothing but a warm glow of satisfaction.

This was *my* town, the people in it were *my* people.

I had been at the *Greybridge Pioneer* but a few weeks, and the memories of the dozens of post-war Hollywood black and white feature films that had made such an impression on me, and, if I was honest with myself, had probably first made me think that journalism may not be such a bad way of earning a crust, had still not faded totally into oblivion.

The heroes were hard-bitten, world-weary figures in battered fedoras, white trenchcoats, and dusty, well-worn shoes, who spent their lives fighting personal campaigns to right the wrongs in their world. They lived a seedy, yet glamorous existence in which the beer flowed steadily, the atmosphere was thick with cigarette smoke - and they always got the girl in the end as a bonus. They could bust a crime syndicate operating out of City Hall, expose a crooked police chief, unmask the most notorious villain, without breaking into a sweat. Celluloid heroes to a man.

The *Greybridge Pioneer* may not have been the *Daily Globe*, or the *Daily Citizen* of fictional fame, but the spirit was the same. The profession.

I was brought back to reality by an urgent clattering as a lone man made his way down the steps to the platform, bicycle slung over one shoulder, canvas bag over the other. He reached the bottom, dropped the bike to the ground, and paused to get his breath back.

He wore the uniform of a railwayman, and he had the lined face of a man who had seen a lot of life, not all good, during his time on this earth, which I estimated at approaching sixty years.

"It'll be warmer on other side," he muttered as he drew level.

"Sheltered from wind."

I dutifully fell into step behind him.

The railwayman propped his bike up against a wooden bench.

"It's been a long day," I said conversationally.

"Aye," he replied.

He let the canvas bag drop from his shoulders and balanced it on the handlebars of his bicycle. He busied himself testing his tyre pressures with a grubby thumb, making no further effort to continue the conversation. Eventually he stood back, apparently satisfied, and sat down beside me on the cold wooden bench.

"Do you work here?" I asked.

"Signal box," he muttered.

"Important job," I said.

He suddenly came to life.

"Bloody important!" he fired back. "But you try telling bosses that."

"Them as pays wages. You try telling them!"

"Then they goes putting in paper railwaymen have got ten per cent rise. Ten per bloody cent. It's all right for these long distance drivers. All right for them."

"And these bosses sat on their fat behinds in their warm offices."

"But what about us?"

"Me and my mates stuck down here. We've got ten per cent all right."

" But what's ten per cent of bugger all? I'll tell you. Bugger all."

"And its freezing in that box, you know."

"And what with Frank turning in half an hour late…"

He stopped to muster his thoughts.

He came to the conclusion, apparently, that I was the last person to understand his predicament.

"I suppose you've been sat in a warm office all day," he said.

I shrugged.

"In and out," I said.

A glimmer of interest appeared in his face.

"So you don't stop in office all time," he said.

I shook my head.

He paused for a minute longer. I thought for one awful moment he wasn't going to actually get round to asking what I did.

"What do you do then?" he asked after what seemed an eternity.

I tugged at the collar of my overcoat, pulling it more snugly round my shoulders and smiled in his direction.

"Newspapers," I said.

I took out a packet of cigarettes.

"Sell them?" he queried.

"No. I don't sell them," I snapped with some disgust.

"I work for one. I'm a journalist."

I took out a Senior Service, tapped the end on the packet, and with an art I had witnessed a hundred times on the silver screen, transferred it with casual disdain to the corner of my mouth.

I put the packet back in my pocket and fished out a box of matches.

"What paper's that then?" came the thin voice from beside me.

I struck a match.

The stiff wind claimed the brief flickering flame before it could catch hold.

"Greybridge Pioneer," I replied, hoping that my tone of voice reflected the years of pride and tradition behind the name.

"That rag," muttered my companion.

I was about to protest, but felt I would be fighting a lost cause. I struck another match. Again it fleetingly spluttered and gave up the struggle.

"What do you do then?"

I glanced at my companion. He seemed more interested in the state of his oily leather boot than in me.

"I told you," I replied. "I'm a journalist."

He nodded understandingly, but his expression remained blank.

I struck a third match, and this time, ducking under my coat, managed to catch the light.

"But what do you do?" my companion repeated, when I had surfaced again.

I drew on the cigarette. This was the prop to complete the image.

The pictures of all those celluloid heroes flashed before my eyes.

"I'm the news editor," I said with pride.

My companion nodded again.

"But what do you *do*?" he persisted, transferring his attention to his other boot.

Where had this man been living during the boom years of the cinema? Under a stone?

I did my best to enlighten him.

I told him about organising the diary, assigning reporters to their tasks, handling the more important stories myself, organising the photographic coverage.

With a final flourish I summed it up rather well, I thought, by outlining my weekly attempts to reflect the life and changing moods of Greybridge. And the only effective way to do that was to have your finger on the pulse of the town twenty-four hours a day.

That was what I did.

My job. My vocation. My life.

I took one last draw on my diminishing cigarette, and with a deft flick sent it curling in a careless arc to come to rest between the railway lines.

I tugged at my coat collar again as I had seen my screen idols do so often before me, and waited for his reaction.

He was testing the tension of the chain on his bicycle. That completed to his satisfaction, he turned his attention back to me, understanding at last reflected in his pale grey eyes.

"I'm with you," he said at last.

"You fill bits between adverts."

I glanced towards the far end of the long viaduct that guarded the eastern end of the town like a dark, praying mantis.

The lights of the local train came into view as it made its way slowly but surely towards the temporary haven of Greybridge Central, a shuffling centipede making steady progress over the back of the soot-blackened edifice that straddled the valley below.

My companion got to his feet, slung his canvas bag over his shoulder, turned his bicycle round and headed for the spot where he knew from years of experience the guard's van would stop.

He had put my life into perspective.

I felt the first spots of chilling rain as I reflected on the reality of my world. My reason for living.

To fill the bits between the adverts.

1

THE damp, grey mist clung to Greybridge like a gossamer veil. The tall spire of St Peter on the Hill, standing sentinel-like at the head of the town, thrust defiantly upwards, its divine erectness penetrating the clammy haze.

Out of the gloom ahead, making its ponderous way along the winding road, loomed the faded, yellow delivery van belonging to the *Greybridge Pioneer*.

The tired old van drew level, paused for breath as the ageing driver changed gear, then, with a roar of relief, settled down to the task in hand once again as it trundled away round the bend and out of view, carrying with it the faded but unmistakeable legend "Greybridge Pioneer. Every Thursday. The Voice of Greybridge".

It wasn't the biggest voice in Greybridge. That dubious honour went to the *Evening Herald Group of Newspapers*, a slick, glossy operation that had sprung up in the post war years on the site of what had been the Home and Colonial Butchery Department until a direct hit wiped it from the face of the earth in September 1943.

But the *Pioneer* had something that the *Evening Herald Group of Newspapers*, with all the trappings of modern technology, would never have. It had roots. It had a history in the town.

The *Pioneer* started life as the *Greybridge and District Gazette* one hundred and twenty years ago, launched by a group of young townsmen with fire in their bellies and a heartfelt need to speak out against what they saw as the social injustices of the day.

On more than one occasion, its very existence came under severe threat as the owners continued to snipe at what they saw were the gross injustices of a small market town having the life blood squeezed out of it by tyrannical landowners.

But to the heavily-taxed townsfolk, the *Gazette* was more than the voice of radicalism. It was a symbol of hope. It had to survive.

One thing the majority of the founders appeared to have in common was a very short life expectancy. One by one, they disappeared from the scene, some in very mysterious circumstances. There was only one exception of note. William Fawcett somehow managed to survive his allotted span of three score years and ten, and end his days in his own bed.

He left three sons and eleven grandchildren to keep the *Gazette* flag

flying. But as the worst of the oppressive laws were repealed, the *Gazette* had less and less to fight for. It became increasingly a recorder of local events, the campaigning newspaper tag fast fading into history, and for many years after the death of William Fawcett, it struggled from one crisis to the next.

But for the *Gazette,* salvation and stability were just over the horizon in the shape of the Greybridge and District Co-op Movement, which eventually took over a controlling interest.

The name was changed from the *Gazette* to the Pioneer, in honour of the Rochdale Pioneers who founded the Co-operative movement, and for the first time in its chequered career it began to actually flourish commercially.

After the dust had settled on the second world war however, it quickly became apparent that power and influence were beginning to drift into new hands.

For those who were prepared to take the gamble, to take up the reins and drive out into the brave new world that was emerging - a world of invention, re-building, modernisation, new technology - the sky was the limit. It was this era that spawned the *Evening Herald* group.

And it was through this era that the *Greybridge Pioneer* proudly held aloft the banner for the old standards. Solid, respectable. Utterly dependable.

In the years following the second world war, there was a generation in control who valued these principles highly. A generation who would resist change to their dying breath, and who would happily part with their last two pence in exchange for a copy of the *Greybridge Pioneer*, which continued to wear its name with pride in an Olde English script, the style of which could not have been more apt if each copy had been carved individually on slate.

But the times, they were a-changing. The local Co-op Movement realised that changes had to be made in the interests of progress if it were to survive. Sadly, there was no place for the *Pioneer* any more in its plans for the future.

So the paper had a new owner. This time a retired haulage contractor who was heading for early retirement.

To James Dalrymple Hogg, the *Pioneer* was the answer to a life-long dream. When he wrote out his cheque to clinch the deal, he bought everything the paper stood for. Respectability. Dependability. In fact all the qualities he could never have hoped to achieve personally.

So with a new owner, the paper sallied forth into the brave new world borne out of the six years of destruction. A new owner who had amassed a vast fortune out of being in the right place at the right time, while his countrymen were sacrificing their lives in his defence.

A new owner who didn't know a thing about newspapers.

Inevitably, the paper slipped into the steady decline of old age and decay, heading quietly for the end that to every sane man in Greybridge, seemed inevitable. But to the formidable James Dalrymple Hogg was unthinkable.

As long as the *Pion*eer existed, he had position and standing in the town. So the answer was simple. He used his vast wealth to keep it from going under.

Then, when he passed onto a higher life, he left the whole operation, including the tiny commercial printing and rubber stamp business, to his only son, Aubrey Dalrymple Hogg, with a specific directive that the *Pioneer* be kept open and running as a commercial enterprise.

Aubrey may well have felt this an unreasonable request had it not been for the fact that his dear father, who it was reputed couldn't even remember his son's name until he was 14, had left enough money in trust to ensure the future of the *Pioneer* for many years to come.

And what's more, he made it a condition of his will that Aubrey would receive nothing unless he made it his business to ensure that the *Greybridge Pioneer* survived.

That was six years ago. Six years before I was to coax my ageing Morris Minor to the top of Greybridge Edge before freewheeling down through the swirling mist to take up my first job in newspapers.

To many better qualified, more worthy entrants into the noble profession of journalism, the faded corner shop with the ill-fitting front door would not have drawn a second glance. Not unless they happened to be engaged in some exposé of slum dwellings, Victorian working conditions, the exploitation of the lower paid, or wanted to put an open and shut case for a drastic policy of urban renewal.

But to a young man in his late teens, with a burning desire to be a journalist since the day he scrawled what was interpreted as a socially unacceptable word on the front room wall with his first crayon, the *Greybridge Pioneer* was the first, firm, concrete step on the road to the promised land.

2

THE first time I set eyes on Walter Charlesworth Piggin - pronounced Pigeon - the esteemed and highly respected editor-in-chief of the Greybridge and District Pioneer Group of Newspapers, his piercing blue eyes were focused on a bluebottle as it made its way hesitatingly across the lid of his plastic lunch box.

I had been directed upstairs to his office by Mrs Barker, a blousy, well-endowed lady the wrong side of 40, with bottle blonde hair the texture of candy floss, and make-up that would have done justice to a time-served plasterer.

Almost before I had a chance to tell her I was the potential new boy, she made it clear to me that she was known as Christine to her friends, as Chris or Chrissy to her closer friends, and, as I subsequently found out, as a pushover to half the male population of Greybridge.

She told me I would find Mr Piggin on the floor above. Not literally - at least not at this time of the day. But that was where his office was located. She advised me to knock before I went in, because that was the way he liked things. It may have been a simple matter had there been a door on his office. There had, of course, *been* a door, but it had somehow disappeared with the passage of time, as had most of the *Pioneer's* circulation.

I stood outside the doorway, watching the legendary W.C. - legendary, that is among the readership of the *Pioneer* - as he carefully rolled up a newspaper and waited for the unsuspecting bluebottle to reach the edge of his plastic lunch box.

I raised my hand to knock on the decaying woodwork, just as he brought the newspaper down with a loud thwack. The bluebottle flew to safety. But the lunch box somersaulted through the air.

"Damn," said the editor, as he scraped the remains of a half-eaten sardine and tomato sandwich off his crumpled pinstriped trousers.

Perhaps this wasn't the best time to make my entrance.

"Damn you," came the voice from the office, its owner's face turning an increasingly deep scarlet, his slim moustache bristling with indignation.

He replaced the plastic lunch box and its gory contents in its allotted place on the desk. Then he straightened his pens, pencils, stapler, hole punch, in-tray, out-tray, rubber stamp tree, rubber stamp pad, paper clip box and finally his telephone.

At last, it seemed, it was safe to make my presence known. I raised my knuckles once again and gave a sharp tap on the door frame. But it was never heard.

The editor had just untwisted the phone cable, and replaced the handset, when it rang.

The urgent jangling was so unexpected, he dropped the phone into his wastepaper basket.

A distant, tiny female voice struggled to get out.

"Hello. Hello…"

Walter Piggin dived into the waste paper basket, and salvaged the receiver from the discarded morning's mail.

He deftly juggled it between fingers coated lightly with sardine and butter, before dropping it again, this time into his sandwich box.

"This is bloody ridiculous," he bellowed.

The insistent female voice stopped instantly.

The editor retrieved the elusive instrument once again, and clamped it firmly against his ear.

This had gone on quite long enough. There was no way he was going to let an inanimate lump of plastic get the better of him.

"Hello," he said with more control. "Walter Piggin speaking. Editor-in-chief of the Pioneer Group of Newspapers."

His expression darkened.

"No, madam. I *don't* have anything to do with classified advertising."

"Put you back to the switchboard?"

"I'll do my best, madam."

"If you should lose us, please ring back."

He slammed the phone down into its cradle and gazed out of the window across the rooftops.

At last, I thought. This is it.

I rapped sharply on the door frame.

This time my efforts didn't go unnoticed.

The editor turned and dropped his voice half an octave.

"Come in," he called.

As I approached his desk, he stood up and held out his podgy little hand towards me. For the first time since I had set eyes on him, his face cracked into a smile. There was warmth and humour in those time-wearied eyes.

"You must be the new lad," he said. "Christine said you were on your way."

Christine, I noted, as I took the proffered hand and shook it warmly. Not Chris. Or Chrissy. That didn't place him very high up on her list of priorities, nor her on his.

"Well take the weight off your feet."

The only chair in the room was about eight feet from the desk. In a corner.

I had no intention of trying to conduct an interview at that range, so I went to move it closer. As I picked it up one of the legs fell off with a clatter.

"Should have warned you about that," said Walter with some concern.

"It's been around nearly as long as I have."

I carried the pieces of chair to the front of the editor's desk.

"And how long has that been?" I asked conversationally.

"Must be 40 years," he reflected. "Man and boy."

"Maybe more. I've stopped counting."

I assembled the chair to the best of my ability.

"Mind you, I'm in better shape than that," he chuckled, the telephone incident now seemingly forgotten.

"At least *my* leg doesn't drop off when somebody picks me up."

7

Once again the eyes radiated warmth and humour.

"Well, then. I suppose I'd better tell you a bit about the job."

"Don't you want to know something about me?" I asked.

He smiled. "It's all in your letter, isn't it? It is all true, I take it."

"That's right," I conceded. "Every word."

"Right then," smiled Walter. "How much do you know about the *Pioneer*?"

I had to admit it wasn't very much. I knew it was a weekly paper. I knew they were advertising for a journalist. I knew I wanted the job.

"Then I'll tell you," said Walter, making himself comfortable in the manner of a man about to discuss his favourite topic over a glass of port.

I was wrong about the port!

*   *   *   *

Some 20 minutes later I was well briefed in the history of the owner, Aubrey Dalrymple Hogg, and his illustrious forebears. And in the traditions of the *Pioneer* in Greybridge, and the need to uphold these fine traditions in the face of intense competition. The intense competition, it was pointed out with some force, came in the main from new technology, a careless abandon of old values and standards, an increasing willingness by some parties to sacrifice service to the community on the altar of high profitability - in a word, the *Herald*.

Having been put straight on that score, I was then treated to a complete run-down on the staff, which took considerably less time than the editor's pronouncements on the evils of the *Herald* group.

This was due, in the main, to the fact that the *Pioneer* didn't seem to be carrying too much excess weight in the engine room.

From what I could gather, the entire editorial staff consisted of an enigma by the name of Elliot Forbes, two reporters, a freelance photographer who turned in when he had nothing better to do, and an advertising and administration department which seemed to outnumber the people who actually produced the paper by about two to one.

With a final thinly-veiled warning that Chris - which he hurriedly amended to Christine - was reputed to eat young men like me for breakfast, the editor stood up and with a flourish said he would show me round. The interview apparently was at an end.

"I hope you don't mind me mentioning this," I said apologetically, as he tried to negotiate the corner of his desk without dislodging any of his carefully positioned trimmings of power. "But there is one question."

He stopped and looked at me.

"I'm sorry," he said. "I thought I'd covered everything."

He sat down heavily in his chair.

"The job," I said.

He raised an eyebrow.

"The job?"

"I was wondering, well what exactly is it? The advertisement just said journalist required."

"That's right," said the editor, looking at me in some puzzlement.

"But what *exactly*," I continued. "It wasn't too specific. Are you looking for a reporter, a sub editor, feature writer?"

"That's right," said the editor.

"But which?" I persisted.

"That depends entirely on you, young man," he beamed at me benevolently.

"That's one thing we're not short of here. Opportunity."

"But what *exactly* are you *looking* for?" I said almost apologetically.

"What exactly were *you* looking for?:" he countered.

"Well, ideally I was hoping to do a bit of reporting." I replied.

"No problem," he interrupted. "Plenty of opportunity for that."

"And the occasional feature?"

"Thursday mornings," said the editor.

"And I wouldn't mind doing a bit of sub editing…"

"Saturday morning, Monday afternoon, all day Tuesday and Wednesday," he said with a beaming smile. "Anything else?"

I couldn't think what to say. I came in search of a job. I seemed to have unearthed an entire business enterprise scheme.

"Whatever your ambitions, you'll be able to realise them with us. Have no fear of that," he said.

"Now if you've no more questions, I'll show you round. Give you a chance to meet one or two people."

He made his way once again gingerly past the corner of his desk.

This time, I didn't stop him.

*   *   *   *

It didn't take long to show me round.

The photographer hadn't been seen all day.

The two younger reporters were out.

And Elliot Forbes was nowhere to be seen, either. He, apparently, was a law unto himself.

The "big room", as it was affectionately known - there appeared to be only two rooms on the editorial floor, and the smaller of the two was occupied by the editor - was completely devoid of human life.

"Never mind," said the editor dismissively. "You'll meet them all in good time."

"So when can you start?"

"A week on Monday," I said quickly.

"You're offering me the job?"

The editor looked at me thoughtfully, and scratched his right ear.

"I've been in this business a long time," he said.

"It may not have made me a wealthy man, but I do pride myself in having gained a considerable insight into the human race. What I'm looking for in the person who'll be filling this very important position within the Pioneer Group of weekly newspapers..."

"I thought there was only the one," I started to interject.

"The Pioneer *Group* of weekly newspapers," intoned the editor forcefully.

"What I'm looking for is someone with integrity, ambition, the ability to express himself clearly and concisely, and above all to maintain the standards our readers have come to expect over the years."

"From what I've seen of you, young man, your letter, your enthusiasm, your keen interest and sympathetic approach towards what we are striving to achieve here week by week, I am convinced you are the man for the job."

"If you want it, the position is yours."

I could feel my chest swelling with pride. It was only when I was outside the building, having bade Walter Piggin a warm farewell, that it occurred to me that we hadn't even mentioned money, holidays, travelling expenses...

I tried to put the thoughts out of my mind.

I had the job!

Working for such a respected group of newspapers and such a revered editor, the rest was bound to take care of itself.

Wasn't it?

*   *   *   *

I decided to have a quick drink to celebrate before starting back home. I crossed the road and went into the lounge bar of the Mitre.

"Half of lager," I smiled as the landlord approached.

I looked around.

The bar was empty but for a man who probably wouldn't see 55 again,

clutching a pint pot at a corner of the bar. He was the nearest thing I'd seen outside a fairy grotto to Father Christmas. He wore a grubby bow tie that, at a guess, had once been a pale blue colour. His shiny, red face peered out from between a shock of white hair, and what had been a thick white beard, now stained yellow from the by-products of his pipe.

"Quiet in here tonight," I observed as I paid.

"Usually is for the first half hour," replied the landlord.

He went to get my change. Father Christmas didn't move.

"Haven't seen you in here before," said the landlord as he returned.

"I haven't been in here before," I said. "But no doubt you'll be seeing quite a lot of me from now on."

The landlord looked at me quizzically.

"I'm starting at the *Pioneer* a week on Monday," I said proudly.

I don't quite know what I expected from the landlord, but a welcoming smile would not have gone amiss.

It was not to be.

"Well I suppose it's your life," he said and moved away.

"Did you say *Pioneer*?" A deep, gentle, dark brown voice came from just behind me. I turned round to come face to face with Father Christmas.

"Er, yes. That's right," I said.

"You'll be the new lad then?"

"That's right."

"Elliot Forbes. Two L's, one T."

He held out a huge hand, the back of which was swathed in white hair.

"Pleased to meet you, Mr Forbes," I said, taking the proffered hand.

"Elliot," came the reply. "They all call me Elliot."

"No doubt the Godfather's told you all about me."

"The Godfather?"

"Pisspot," replied Elliot. "W.C."

I smiled.

"He didn't say much about anybody. Except himself."

"What exactly do you do?"

Elliot Forbes shrugged. "You name it." He looked me up and down.

"So what did he tell you about the job?"

"Well it seems he's looking for something of an all-rounder…"

"One-man frigging band more like," said Elliot. "Same as the rest of us."

"The editor gave me the impression that I could have a bright future with the *Pioneer*," I ventured.

"That's right," said Elliot, shifting his ample weight from one foot to the other.

I was not quite sure whether he was agreeing that I could have a bright future with the paper, or merely that it was the impression the editor had given me.

I was rapidly beginning to feel that there was nothing in this world that Elliot Forbes hadn't seen or done in his lifetime.

"I'm sure he meant it," I said, partly in self-defence.

"I'm sure he did," replied Elliot.

"He must have been impressed with my letter. He seemed ready to offer me the job before he'd even met me."

Elliot drained his pint pot.

"He was."

I allowed myself a little smile of self satisfaction.

"You were the only applicant," he sighed, as he pushed his empty glass in my direction.

3

ELLIOT Forbes' comments about one-man bands proved to be very true, as I soon found out. The staff was spread fairly thin on the ground. Apart from Elliot Forbes and myself there were only two other people working in the big room.

Dawn was tall, slim, dark haired and 20. She was also practical and a very reliable reporter. She had left Greybridge County High School with a couple of obscure O-levels four years before. But what she lacked in academic ability, she more than made up for in common sense and an awareness of what was going on around her. And her most endearing feature - she got on with people. She looked after a couple of the country districts, and the womens' organisations.

Gary was two years older than Dawn. A dark, thick-set six-footer, he had left school at 18 with 10 good O-levels, six A-levels and an ego as big as the Town Hall clock tower. He had turned up his nose at the thought of going to university. After some 14 years at school, 10 of them as a boarder, he had seen enough of academic life to last him a lifetime. Now he was ready to take on the world.

The Greybridge and District Pioneer Group of Newspapers was merely a stepping stone on his way to the top. Though the more I got to know this academic genius, who would have had difficulty buttering a piece of bread when it came to practicalities, the more I couldn't help feeling that as far as he was concerned, the Greybridge and District Pioneer was the top - at least as far as the newspaper world was concerned.

I didn't meet Phil the photographer until towards the end of the third week. He had been on holiday in Tenerife, and he came in to have a glance through the diary to see what he had on that weekend.

It had been worth the wait. It was cabaret time as soon as Phil walked through the door, dressed in black shirt and white trousers, and wearing dark glasses, a tan that put him two shades lighter than a block of Cadbury's Dairy Milk, and enough chains round his neck to refurbish the entire W.C. complex under the bus station.

Phil had possibly the best job in Greybridge, if not the country. He was a freelance photographer, but he had a dark room on the *Pioneer* premises equipped with the latest in developing, printing and facsimile transmission technology.

This had come about as the result of an astute business move by his father, who had occupied the position with the newspaper before him, when the then-owner was going through one of his more acute financial difficulties.

Phil's father, who was on the staff at the time, had offered to leave the payroll and provide all the pictures on a freelance basis to ease the financial burden in at least one area. The grateful owner had jumped at the offer, holding Phil's father in very high esteem from that day onward.

As the *Pioneer* climbed back towards one of its rare financial peaks, Phil's father was implored to rejoin the staff, at a remuneration that would reflect the owner's gratitude. But he turned it down. He would continue to be paid just for what he supplied, but if the *Pioneer* really wanted to show its gratitude, it could build and equip a darkroom for him to use, provide office accommodation, telephone and all the other trappings essential to a business life of comparative luxury.

This would benefit both parties of course, as the equipment would always belong to the paper, as Phil's father was quick to point out. He was merely the custodian, and of course, would continue to supply pictures for the paper on a freelance basis.

After Phil had taken over the reins from his father, he was not slow to realise the possibilities.

On the grounds that he was saving the paper money by only charging them for the work he did, he had managed to modernise the dark room, with every conceivable piece of photographic equipment known to man, a small studio area, office, use of telephone, at a cost of not a penny to himself.

The arrangement had its compensations for the rest of us.

Phil fancied himself as a bit of a glamour photographer, and there was a constant stream of local talent parading in and out of his studio.

He seemed to have contacts with every club in the town, which guaranteed us free entry. And if you ever wanted a ticket for a special event, Phil was the boy to see.

Anything from the F.A. Cup Final to a Buckingham Palace garden party, Phil reckoned he could get it.

If only we could get him to show as much enthusiasm for the paper once in a while…

If it hadn't been for his assistant, his son Martin - Phil obviously believed in keeping a good thing in the family - I doubt whether the *Pioneer* would have published a picture from one year's end to the next.

*　　*　　*　　*

If anyone ever doubted that a little learning can be a dangerous thing, they never worked at the *Greybridge Pioneer*.

One of the first things I learned after joining the *Pioneer* was never to admit to a special knowledge of, or interest in, anything.

I hadn't been working there longer than a fortnight, when the editor wandered into the office, clutching the morning mail, casually humming what I vaguely recognised as *Three Little Maids from School*.

"Gilbert and Sullivan fan, eh?" I said conversationally.

The editor stopped in mid hum, and glanced up as if just aroused from a deep sleep.

"Mmm?" he queried.

"Gilbert and Sullivan," I said.

A warm smile flooded the editor's face.

I heard Gary splutter in the corner.

W.C. looked at me like a benevolent uncle.

"It's such a thrill these days to come across a devotee of real music," he said.

"I've always enjoyed Gilbert and Sullivan," I said.

"Splendid," said the editor. "Then this will be right up your street."

He held out a letter headed Greybridge and District Amateur Operatic Society. It informed us that they were doing *The Mikado* the following week at the Civic Theatre.

"We usually go down to get a picture at the dress rehearsal on Tuesday for next week's paper," the editor informed me.

"Then we'll do a review of the show on Saturday."

"And you want me to do the review," I said resignedly, realising I was giving up yet another Saturday night.

"Who better?" beamed the editor.

"Go down to the dress rehearsal with Phil. Make yourself known."

"They'll be glad to see you."

And with a little smile of satisfaction, he turned and went back to his own office.

I turned to Gary as soon as the editor left.

"Am I the *only* one in this office who has ever heard of Gilbert and Sullivan?"

He grinned across at me.

"You're the only one daft enough to admit it," he said.

*   *   *   *

I picked up Phil about seven o'clock on the Tuesday evening. His car, it seemed, was off the road again. It was surprising how often his car was off the road when he went on a job with me.

15

"Think about the expenses, old fruit," he would say.

True, I did claim mileage - pittance though it was.

But so too did he!

After stops at the Orinoco Club (to pick up a couple of tickets - for what, I never knew) and to the Blue Cockatoo (to drop off a couple of tickets) we eventually arrived at the Civic Theatre at ten past eight. We were immediately met by a gushing, middle-aged lady of ample proportions with a lilac hue to her thinning hair, who I later learned was Mrs Farrow.

"We thought you were never coming," she hissed through thin, tight lips, somehow managing to smile at the same time.

Phil walked straight past her, looking intently at the flimsy set.

I thought I'd better introduce myself.

"I'm..."

But I was cut off before I could utter another word about who I was or what I was doing there by the sharp staccato clapping of Mrs Lilac Rinse. The hubbub of conversation round the room stopped as if the sound had been switched off.

"Come along everyone," trilled Mrs Lilac Rinse. "Now we all know our positions."

The assembled company moved at a brisk trot to line-up on the stage.

"The sooner we get this over, the sooner we can begin."

Phil shot off a couple of group pictures of the cast, then took the principals to one side.

"These aren't for the paper," I overheard him say. "But while you're in costume, I thought you might like a couple for yourselves."

"In colour of course. I'll send you a price list with the contacts."

Before they could ask any further questions, he had herded them to the side of the stage, and was weaving this way and that, every flash clicking through his cash-register mind.

Mrs Lilac Rinse, watching with some disapproval, decided to give up the unequal battle and turned her attention to me.

"You're from the newspaper, too?"

"That's right," I agreed. "I'm..."

Once again I was silenced in mid-utterance, as a brow-beaten, slightly-built lady who looked at first sight to be at least 60, but on closer examination was probably nearer 40, burst through the door.

"Mrs Farrow," she said. "I'm sorry. I've got some terrible news."

Mrs Lilac Rinse braced herself to face the intrusion.

"Not now, Ida. Can't you see I'm dealing with the Press?" she trilled, with the same tone she may have used if she was dealing with a plague of cockroaches, or an invasion of Javanese tree frogs.

"I can give you five minutes, young man. If there's anything you want to ask me about the show…"

But Ida wouldn't be silenced.

"Mrs Farrow. Please!" she persisted.

"Not now, Ida," thundered the mighty one.

"Do I have to remind you who is running this show?"

But dear Ida held her ground superbly in the face of the onslaught.

"I know perfectly well who's running it, Mrs Farrow."

"But if you don't listen to me, you won't *have* a show to run."

Mrs Farrow's thin lips started to tremble.

"What are you talking about?" she barked.

"It's Mr Bancroft," said Ida. "He's gone down with flu."

Mrs Farrow looked as if she had been hit between the eyes by a number 33 bus.

"But he can't," she said. "*He can't!*"

"He has," Ida insisted.

"This is terrible," said Mrs Farrow, her brashness fast disappearing into genuine concern.

"It's not that bad," I offered in a bid to drag her out of her misery.

"This particular strain rarely lasts for more than 48 hours."

"I'm not talking about the flu," she rasped. "It's the show."

"How can you do *The Mikado* without a pianist?"

She had a problem, I had to admit.

"Surely there's someone…"

"Not like Mr Bancroft," wailed the hapless Mrs Farrow.

I shook my head in sympathy.

"And it isn't as if you could bring in any old pianist is it? Not at this late stage"

She shot me a withering glance.

"What do you know about it?"

"I did take piano lessons for four years," I volunteered in my own defence.

I didn't tell her I could play no better at the end of my four years than I could at the beginning, with the possible exception of a stilted version of the *Blue Danube*.

Her face lit up.

"My dear boy. I'm sure with a bit of practice it will all come back to you."

"If you just picked out the right hand for tonight, and put in a bit of practice tomorrow."

I suddenly realised what she was getting at.

"Me?" I said in astonishment.

"Oh, no. There's no way I can play for you."

She was not to be shaken off easily.

"Nonsense," she said. "You must have learned something."

I had. I'd learned that if I practised until Lundy Island won the World Cup I'd still never make a pianist.

"It wasn't entirely my idea," I said meekly.

"My aunt was the musical one of the family."

"Your aunt?" said Mrs Farrow with interest.

"That's right. She could play anything," I volunteered as I looked round desperately for Phil.

"That's what got me interested," I babbled. "It was only when I tried for myself that I realised it was a gift. Some people have it, some don't."

I caught sight of Phil and beckoned him over.

"I think we'd better be moving," I said.

"You can't leave us like this," said Mrs Farrow.

"We're in a desperate situation. And you're probably the only person who can help us."

"I can't. Honestly," I said.

"If I could just say something," volunteered Phil.

I thought for a minute he was about to do a rescue act for which I would be eternally grateful.

"If you and Mrs Farrow have things to discuss, don't mind me. I can find my own way back."

"We haven't," I yelled.

But Phil was halfway to the door.

"Phil!" I screeched after him.

But he swung the door behind him and he was gone.

I turned back to face Mrs Farrow.

"Look, I realise what a desperate situation you're in," I said.

"But I could never play the piano well enough to accompany *The Mikado* if I practised from now until next Christmas."

"Of course not," agreed Mrs Farrow.

"Silly of me to suggest it."

The relief flooded through me. It was short-lived.

"Tell me. Where does your aunt live?"

* * * *

Aunt Meg lived about five miles out of Greybridge, the last mile and a quarter along an unmade road that disappeared into the cart track that led to the smallholding she shared with Uncle Frank.

Mrs Farrow insisted on coming with me.

I readily agreed. With Mrs Farrow by my side, I could see this latest crisis in my life coming to an end sooner rather than later. If Uncle Frank didn't give this arrogant shrew her marching orders, I was convinced Aunt Meg would.

I was out of luck.

Uncle Frank was out at the pub.

And Aunt Meg got on with Mrs Farrow like wildfire. Before I could fully grasp the situation, I was ferrying them both back to the Civic Theatre to start the rehearsal.

"I'm glad it's worked out," I called to Mrs Farrow, after I had deposited her and Aunt Meg back at the Civic Theatre.

"I'll look forward to seeing the show on Saturday."

"You're not going?" said Aunt Meg in surprise.

"There's nothing for me to stay for now," I shrugged.

Aunt Meg looked at me and blinked behind the thick lenses of her spectacles, which made her eyes look twice their normal size.

"But who's going to turn the music for me?" she asked.

I felt my heart sink into my shoes.

"You don't expect me..." I started to protest.

"Good man," said Mrs Farrow. "I don't know what we'd have done without you." She surveyed her assembled troubadours.

"Right boys and girls. Take your cue from the piano. Now from the top..."

The next four nights were the longest of my life.

Mrs Farrow loved every minute. Aunt Meg was in raptures.

The cast enjoyed themselves immensely, and the audiences were well pleased. After the final show on the Saturday night, Mrs Farrow was most generous in her praise for the company, for Aunt Meg, and surprisingly, me.

"Without the help of our friend here from the *Herald*..."

"*Pioneer*," I corrected.

"We may never have had a show," she said appreciatively.

I never ceased to marvel that this domineering lady, who could remember with great accuracy every line of whatever musical she happened to be working on, never did get round to remembering my name.

* * * *

On Monday morning, I heard the heavy footsteps of Walter Piggin on the landing as he crossed from his office to the big room.

Dawn was trying to decipher the notes of a meeting she had been to.

Gary hadn't yet turned in. I grabbed the nearest daily paper to hand, and dived into the welcome haven of its pages.

The editor was humming quietly to himself as he came into the room. It sounded like a cross between an unauthorised version of the *National Anthem* and the *Muskrat Ramble*.

"Had Mrs Farrow on the phone to me at home yesterday," he said without looking up from the clutch of mail in his hand.

I quietly emerged from the depths of page five.

"She couldn't speak highly enough of you," he continued.

"You've made a friend for life there."

I lowered the paper further.

Dawn shot me a grin across the room.

The editor dropped the mail on Elliot Forbes' desk. He turned to leave. He hummed a couple more bars of his musical offering. I tried again to make it out. I think *Muskrat Ramble* just won on points.

He stopped in the doorway and turned back.

"I don't suppose you know anything about jazz, do you?"

"Not a thing," I replied emphatically.

"Mmm. Pity," said the editor.

"Sorry," I continued.

"Don't be," he said. "No problem. Gary will do it."

I smiled contentedly to myself as the editor went back to his office.

I was learning. Never admit anything.

And that's how I came to miss out on the greatest two-day jazz festival Greybridge had ever known!

4

THE Union Canal threaded its way through Greybridge like an abandoned ribbon draped casually across a slag heap. It brought some colour to the town, that couldn't be denied. A brownish orange to be exact, its still waters tainted over the years by a miscellany of waste products from the industry that had once sat proudly astride its banks, and which had at one time been the life blood of the town.

It brought colour in other ways, too. Every June, there was a Festival of Boats, when, for a whole week, boat buffs from the length and breadth of the country converged on the old basin and transformed it into an explosion of colourful activity.

For the rest of the summer, there was a constant stream of narrow boats and other small craft passing through the town. Very few bothered to stop. And during the winter, the water-borne traffic ceased altogether. It was at this time of the year that the activity spread to the canal banks, and to be more precise, to the derelict buildings that still managed to stand despite the ravages of time.

Many of them had expired years ago, but there were still the odd one or two that were windproof, water-proof and comparatively private, which seemed to sum up all the amenities the more amorous residents of the town sought for their illicit activities, on a dark, dank Saturday night after closing time.

My pre-occupation with the Union Canal started almost immediately I started work at the *Pioneer*. It was difficult to ignore it, as it ran along the back of the *Pioneer* building.

Many was the day I would peer down into the murky brown waters in search of inspiration, but the dismal, uninspired view served only to dull what senses were left.

Directly across the canal, nestling cosily beside the lower reaches of the Commercial Road bridge, was the Hope Street Wesleyan Chapel, with its more modern community centre tucked guardedly under its protective wing.

Hope Street Wesleyan Chapel had for years been the spiritual, cultural and social centre to the vast majority of Greybridge's god-fearing inhabitants, despite the presence of St Peter's, Our Lady's, St Columba's, Presbyterian and more recently, the Church of Latter Day Saints.

It was a place to meet, to talk, to see and be seen. Whether it be youth club, W.I., Flower Guild, Young Wives, Rotarians, or members of the several mysterious lodges that abounded, with their secret rituals and built-in respectability.

It was part of the very fabric on which Greybridge had been built.

If there was one man who typified the activities of the Hope Street Methodist Chapel it would have to be Councillor Bramwell Unsworth, purveyor of high class fruit, flowers and vegetables, floral tributes and arrangements made up to order.

Councillor Bramwell Unsworth was an expansive man in every sense of the word.

He was well over six feet tall, carrying enough spare flesh to keep him well warm in winter. His close-cropped, military-style moustache, intended to give him an air of authority, no doubt, only succeeded in accentuating the size of his ample nose. While his shock of near white hair made him look much more advanced than his 53 years.

Every Sunday morning, his voice could be heard booming from the pulpit, where, as a lay preacher, he laid down the moral tone for the faithful to follow during the coming week.

On a fine summer's day, his words would waft out of the open front door, a constant reminder to nearby residents should they need it that it was but an hour to opening time.

For the rest of the week, he would be going about his council business, making Greybridge a better place in which to live, while the actual business of running the shop and earning a crust was left in the capable hands of his wife, little Mrs Emmeline Unsworth.

And a very effective councillor he was too. He was instrumental in having a waste bin moved 20 yards along Commercial Road. And in stopping the proprietor of the Chinese takeaway next to the gas works from putting up an illuminated shop sign advertising the fact that he was there, on the grounds that it would detract from the visual amenities of the area.

But perhaps his most noteworthy feat was organising the erection of a sign on the little park at the back of the bus station, which had been used for all manner of things since time immemorial, stating that it was a public amenity for the pleasure of everyone. Then going on to ban ball games, dog walking, horse riding, and urging people to keep off the grass.

When visitors came to Greybridge and rapidly arrived at the conclusion that there would probably be more excitement in watching the grass grow, at least they now had a place to put this statement to the test.

Thanks to the untiring efforts of Councillor Unsworth, it was the only activity permitted!

But one glance was sufficient to tell the casual observer that this tall, erect figure was one of the pillars of Greybridge society. Guardian of all that was worth preserving in the town.

At least, through his own eyes. To the rest of us, he had all the appeal and attraction of a boil on the backside.

*   *   *   *

My introduction to him was brief and to the point, following a council meeting shortly after my arrival at the *Pioneer*.

He took me to one side, one huge paw of a hand cupped in fatherly embrace on my shoulder, to explain that everything he stood for in the council chamber was correct, and everyone else who represented the electorate of Greybridge was an ill-informed, mis-directed moron.

I grunted a vague reply through a mouthful of chocolate digestive biscuit and council coffee, which he took to be a mark of agreement. Consequently, from that day on, he promised to keep me one step ahead of events of significant local importance as he could see I was a man of profound intelligence and unswerving integrity.

True to his word, Councillor Unsworth became a frequent visitor to the *Pioneer* offices. Elliot Forbes positively encouraged it.

"You've dropped on your feet there, laddie. Your own personal contact inside the corridors of power."

"Takes some years to achieve that. If ever."

"Takes a man of..." he hesitated while he sought the right words.

"Intelligence and integrity?" I ventured.

"Precisely," he beamed.

I was about to ask why no one else had struck up such a relationship. After all, the Councillor had been around long before I arrived on the scene.

But the benevolent Elliot suddenly discovered a more pressing engagement.

It didn't take me long, either, to notice that whenever the revered Councillor's booming voice announced his arrival in the front office, Gary and Dawn had the happy knack of disappearing like bathwater.

But Councillor Unsworth didn't seem to notice or care.

After all, wasn't I the one with the integrity and intelligence?

Several times a week I would receive Councillor Unsworth, to hear of his latest achievement on behalf of the fortunate population of Greybridge and district.

But gradually, my enthusiasm for the relationship began to wane, particularly after he found it necessary to phone me at three o'clock one morning after he had returned from one of his lodge meetings to inform me

23

that he had decided to press ahead for a total ban on dogs in Greybridge Memorial Park.

This apparently arose out of an unfortunate incident as the Councillor, in half-intoxicated state - he didn't drink, merely took wine with the various fellowships to which he belonged - was crossing the memorial park one night, stumbled and had an altercation with a sizeable lump of canine excrement.

He announced in unfaltering tones that at the next meeting of the council, not only would he press for the introduction of a bye law banning all dogs from the park immediately, but he would also press for notices to this effect to be erected around the perimeter as a matter of urgency.

I couldn't help thinking what the illiterate, unaccompanied dogs of the borough would make of that!

*   *   *   *

The office visits settled down quite quickly into a pattern.

Two, sometimes three mornings a week, Councillor Unsworth would honour us with his presence.

Elliot Forbes would make his excuses and leave.

Gary and Dawn would find pressing things to do elsewhere.

Only Christine in the front office would offer any more than a brief greeting to the man.

I almost began to feel sorry for Councillor Bramwell Unsworth.

Some two months after I first met the revered Councillor, I was ploughing through the minutes for the following week's council meeting, when one item in particular caught my eye.

It concerned Wharf Street, which ran along the other side of the canal, from the Commercial Road bridge to Gladstone Street.

At one time, the area had been the bustling centre of commercial activity in the town, as the barges loaded and unloaded their colourful wares. But now it was nothing more than a festering sore. There were a couple of old warehouses still standing, now partially converted into industrial premises of various sizes, and a couple of shops where Wharf Street joined Gladstone Street.

Whatever else had adorned the canal bank in years past had slipped quietly into history, as decay had taken its toll.

One of the shops belonged to a newsagent, Sam Greatbanks, who seemed older than the wharf itself.

While the corner shop had been turned into a council information centre, where Councillor Unsworth and his two ward colleagues held their surgeries every third Saturday morning.

Now it was being mooted that the occupants of the warehouses should be offered incentives to move to an industrial estate on the other side of town, that Sam Greatbanks be offered whatever inducement he considered reasonable to vacate his premises, and that the whole area be razed to the ground and landscaped - an unquestionable and long overdue improvement.

The following morning, Councillor Unsworth arrived to let me know that he had attended a meeting of his constituency committee the previous evening, and official policy was to oppose any plans for a Greybridge by-pass. As there were no plans for a Greybridge by-pass, and were not likely to be in my lifetime, this seemed a singularly uninteresting piece of useless information.

But as the Councillor said, it was a question of attitudes.

"We need to let the people of this town know that we are constantly vigilant," he announced with considerable dignity.

"Whatever the threat, we are ready, willing and able to combat it."

I offered him a cup of coffee. He refused. He had to be on his way.

He was halfway to the door when I remembered there was something I had to ask him.

"Er...Councillor. There was one thing..."

Councillor Unsworth stopped in his tracks and turned, waiting for me to go on.

"Wharf Street," I said.

He pulled himself up to his full height. His moustache bristled with indignation.

"Wharf Street?" he repeated quizzically. "What about it?"

"You've seen the minutes for the next council meeting. It's coming up for discussion. I take it you're in favour of the scheme?"

The Councillor went two shades darker.

"In favour of the scheme! Some crackpot idea put forward by a bunch of radical Johnnie Nobodies that will destroy our very heritage? Are you out of your mind, boy?"

I was completely taken aback by this outburst.

Could this be the forward-thinking, upstanding man of the people talking?

"But it's an eyesore," I ventured. "A throwback from a by-gone age."

"If this plan went through, it would open up the whole canal basin as a pleasant amenity for the town."

Councillor Unsworth was shaking visibly.

"Didn't they teach you anything at school about values?" he thundered.

"About the need to conserve, to preserve our heritage?"

"To show pride in the work of our forebears. Or are you one of these radical Johnnie Knowalls too, who think they can get away with any sort of urban vandalism in the name of progress?"

"I'm sorry," I said. "But if there is anything aesthetically pleasing about a rotting pile of bricks and mortar, a few derelict buildings and a breeding ground for rats..."

"Listen, laddie," the Councillor thundered. "Have you any idea how much this landscaping scheme is going to cost? Have you?"

I had no more idea than I had of the price of best haddock in Heligoland. I shook my head.

"One hell of a lot, believe me. Money that this town can ill afford. There are far better ways of spending it than destroying part of our heritage, believe me."

And as far as he was concerned, that was that. He turned on his heel and was gone.

I heard a hurried exchange between the Councillor and Christine, then the glass rattling in the front door as it was slammed.

When Councillor Bramwell Unsworth felt strongly about something, he certainly didn't believe in hiding his feelings.

Perhaps he had something. Perhaps there were better ways of spending ratepayers' money than on destroying part of the town's heritage.

Like erecting signs in the memorial park warning the dogs to keep out.

*   *   *   *

The council meeting came and went, without incident.

The matter of landscaping the Wharf Street site came up briefly, but by then, Councillor Unsworth had mustered all the support he needed. The move was rapidly thrown out.

For the foreseeable future, Wharf Street would stand as a monument to a bygone age.

But despite his protestations about the rape of inner cities that was taking place under the banner of progress, I still couldn't understand why Councillor Unsworth felt so strongly about this particular eyesore.

The following Thursday, I had to go along to the Town Hall to cover a presentation of road safety certificates to children from local primary schools. It wasn't worth going home then coming back again. I had a quick toasted sandwich at the Mitre and went back to the office to write up my notes from a general purposes committee meeting the previous evening.

I hadn't got far into my report, when I came across an item concerning a plea for a pelican crossing, which had the feel of a good campaigning story if I could get a couple of quotes from councillors to help it along. I dialled Councillor Unsworth's number.

"Hello," came the thin voice tentatively as the phone was answered.

"Mrs Unsworth?" I inquired.

"That's right."

"I wonder if I could speak to Councillor Unsworth? It's the *Pioneer*."

"I'm sorry," she said almost apologetically. "He's out. And I don't know what time he'll be back. It's his lodge night tonight, you see."

"Really?" I said in some surprise. "I thought that was Tuesday night."

"It was...I mean it still is," said Mrs Unsworth, her voice apparently gaining in confidence the more she spoke.

She probably wasn't used to being allowed to go on uninterrupted for so long.

"But just recently, they've changed it to two nights a week. Something to do with the induction of the new Grand Master, you know."

"I see," I said. "Well not to worry. I'll try to catch him tomorrow."

Mrs Unsworth sighed at the other end of the phone.

The conversation had probably been the highlight of an otherwise eventless evening.

"I'll tell him you called," she said.

"Thank you. Goodnight Mrs Unsworth."

"Goodnight."

The phone was put down at the other end. I glanced at my watch. Seven-fifteen. The lodge meetings were held in the Methodist Church Hall crush room. Perhaps if I hurried over I might just catch him.

Then again, I might just miss the start of the road safety presentation. I put Councillor Unsworth out of my mind, turned out the light and let myself out of the office.

* * * *

I was held up at the Town Hall longer than I expected. It was turned half past ten when I left, stricken with hunger. I drove round to the chip shop in Gladstone Terrace, pulling up outside just in time to catch the tail end of the crowd from the Tatton, where the film had finished ten minutes before. I had to wait nearly twenty minutes to get served.

When I got back to the car, I turned the key in the ignition only to be greeted by a slow cough, then nothing. I'd left the headlights on, and the battery, far past the prime of its life, had found it all too much.

I turned off the lights, climbed out of the car and headed for the phone box, keeping my fingers crossed that Gary would be in.

He was. He wasn't too pleased to hear from me, but yes, he would come out and give me a jump start. Give him ten minutes.

If I knew Gary that meant half an hour at least.

Chips in hand, I strolled down towards Wharf Street, thinking evil thoughts about car batteries.

When I reached the canal, I stopped, leaned against the railings and looked back across at the old buildings that were strung out along the other side of the street like an uneven row of bad teeth, giving no outward indication of the activities that no doubt were going on in the secrecy of the cobbled alleyways and darkened doorways and loading bays. The panting activity of amorous couples who sought refuge there to snatch a brief moment of frantic bliss, pausing only to hold their breath as they heard approaching footsteps along the road, hoping against hope it wasn't the friendly neighbourhood copper.

I screwed the chip paper into a ball and punted it high in the dark direction of the brooding waters of the canal, before turning back towards Gladstone Street.

As I moved to cross the road, my eye was drawn to the side of the dilapidated shop that served as the council information centre.

I thought I saw a light flash on and off in one of the back windows. But I couldn't have done. Not at that time of night.

It must have been the fleeting reflection of a car's headlights.

I carried on walking back.

I was no more than a dozen yards away from the front door of the darkened doorway of the information centre, when I heard an almost imperceptible click as a door was shut.

I froze.

Perhaps I had seen a light. But why would anyone want to break into the information centre?

Before I could come up with an answer, I saw a shadowy figure emerge from the doorway, pause briefly then hurry away into the darkness of the night.

There was no mistaking the solid frame, the shock of white hair, bristling moustache and the bulbous nose of the esteemed Councillor Bramwell Unsworth.

Was there no end to the devotion to duty of the man?

But if Councillor Unsworth's presence had been a surprise, it was nothing to the one I was about to get.

I was about to set off again towards my stricken car, when a second shadowy figure emerged from the doorway. A much slighter, female form.

She turned towards me, head bowed against the rising wind and any risk of recognition.

There was something familiar about the brown coat, the headscarf with the paisley motifs. And something unmistakeable about the heavy perfume as she hurried past.

"Goodnight, Christine." I said softly.

The clip-clopping of her heels on the pavement stopped. She turned, and looked at me quizzically, without shame.

"How long have you been there?"

"Long enough," I said. "See you in the morning."

I didn't catch her reply. The calm of the evening was shattered by a screech of tyres, squeal of brakes and a long blast on the horn from the direction of the chip shop.

Gary had arrived. I hurried away.

The next morning, Christine was her usual bright and breezy self, making no reference at all to the previous night.

But she did spend some time on the phone to Unsworth's, purveyors of high class fruit, flowers and vegetables, floral tributes and arrangements made up to order, where Councillor Bramwell Unsworth appeared to have suddenly rekindled his interest in the family business to the exclusion of practically everything else.

At least, I assume that was the explanation. It was some time before he showed his face in the *Pioneer* offices again.

5

WALTER Charlesworth Piggin looked out of his grimy office window on to Victoria Street, or what bit of it was still visible. Cars were parked bumper to bumper on either side. Traffic going away from the town waited patiently as a bus disgorged its passengers and then swallowed up the lengthy queue of shoppers and schoolchildren, homeward bound after the trials of another day.

The traffic going the other way, into town, meandered slowly along at little more than a walking pace.

"There's a whole world out there," he said at last.

I solemnly nodded agreement. No one could dispute the fact.

"And it's our world," went on our revered editor.

Now that was open to conjecture.

"Our world?" I repeated, for want of something better to say. I felt his remark invited some comment.

"Our world," he repeated.

He turned and strolled purposefully back to his desk. Well, as purposefully as any man could with chilblains and a bunion the size of a crab apple.

I strolled over to the window and looked down on the activity below.

W.C. sat down behind his desk, straightened his blotter and moved his stapler all of one eighth of an inch to the left of where it was.

"I suppose there is," I said.

My editor was now engrossed in trying to remove a stain from his pullover with the middle finger of his left hand.

"What was that?" he said without looking up.

"I said I suppose there is," I repeated.

"What?" he asked, his attention still on the stain, which was proving more stubborn to move than he had thought.

"A whole world out there," I said.

"Exactly," said Walter, with a final brush at the offending blemish.

"And what are we doing about it?"

I tried to think of a constructive answer. I suppose my contribution ended at paying my taxes.

I was about to volunteer this information, when he saved me the bother.

"I'll tell you," he went on. "Precious little, that's what."

"All those people you can see down there..."

I glanced out of the window. By now the congestion had eased considerably. There was an old lady coming out of the butcher's and a couple of boys on their way home from school pulling faces at the portly senior clerk in the travel agent's.

"…are potential readers of the *Pioneer*," went on Walter.

All three of them, I thought. What potential this paper has.

Walter wasn't finished.

"And what are we doing about it?" he said again.

I opened my mouth to remind him of the newsgathering operation that ensured the *Pioneer* brought to the good folk of Greybridge their weekly ration of local news, views and opinion. But I never got the chance.

"Bugger all," said the editor. And to emphasise the fact he picked up the telephone receiver and let it drop down behind the desk, allowing the cord to unravel.

"We sit in here gleaning what we can from the council minutes. Or on the end of the 'phone. We should be out there. Among the people who count in this world of ours. People like to read about other people. That's what generates the emotions. Tugs at the heartstrings. That's what sells papers. I mean who the devil gives a fig whether the council is going to open a new public convenience in the shopping precinct or not?"

Obviously the words of a man who has never been caught short in the Post Office queue.

"That's not what sells newspapers," he growled.

"People. That's what sells newspapers."

He wasn't wrong. I must have passed three or four of them every night on my way home on different street corners.

"Well? Do you agree or don't you?"

I agreed. I agreed with everything he said as long as he was paying my wages.

"Well just bear it in mind," he said. "And let's see more of it in the paper."

"We're not going to beat the *Herald* unless we get some good human interest stories."

We wouldn't beat the *Herald* if we gave ten copies of our paper away free with every one sold. But I thought it was better to keep this snippet of information to myself for the moment.

My tea was getting cold in the other office, my left foot was beginning to tingle as the inactivity began to take its toll.

"I don't know what's brought this on," I said at last. "But if it's something I've done…"

"You," the editor looked apologetic.

"You don't think I'm getting at you?"

"Well, I was beginning to get the distinct feeling", I replied.

"Good heavens, no. It's the others I'm talking about."

"Gary. And the girl. And the lad in there."

The lad was Elliot Forbes.

"They're the ones who should know better."

"Sitting on their fat behinds in there doesn't sell papers."

"The most creative thing they do in a week is their expenses claim."

"Don't think I don't know what's going on behind my back, right under my nose."

"If you don't mind my asking, why are you telling me and not them?" I asked.

"What's that?" asked the editor.

His attention was now turned to his top right hand drawer, where he seemed to be hunting for something.

"About what sells papers," I said. "If they're the ones who need telling."

"Waste of time," said the editor. "Beyond redemption. I just don't want you falling into the same trap. Complacency."

"You're new to the game. Bright, intelligent. Not tarnished by cynicism. I've got great hopes of you." He fumbled about in the back of the drawer.

"Just you think on," he said. "People."

"That's what sells papers," I volunteered.

He beamed.

I wasn't sure whether it was because I appeared to be on his wavelength, or because he had at last found what he was searching for.

"Every morning when you come in, look out of the window and say to yourself, that is the world of the *Pioneer*."

"That is the reason for our very existence."

He extracted his arm from the drawer. Clutched in his fist was a half-open packet of biscuits.

"Custard cream?" he offered.

"No thanks," I said. "I'd better get back."

He bit into a custard cream, the interview obviously over. As I turned to leave, I glanced out the window at this wonderful world that was so eagerly hanging on my every word.

A black and white Jack Russell sniffed at the billboard outside the newsagents, cocked its leg up, relieved its bladder and walked nonchalantly away.

*   *   *   *

On the other side of Victoria Street from the *Pioneer* office, nestling

snugly between the shops, was the front entrance to what had been originally Victoria Street Mixed Infants.

It had long since ceased to function as a school and its present role was that of hardware and do-it-yourself store, for which it was ideal. There was still a flagged playground between the front of the school and the pavement, which came in very handy for displaying anything from clothes posts to loft ladders for six days a week.

But on Sunday, it looked once again like the little Victoria Street Mixed Infants school of bygone days, save for the small sign proclaiming it was now run by Ashley Hardcastle, ironmonger and purveyor of household wares.

I hadn't really paid that much attention to the frontage of Victoria Street Mixed Infants until one Sunday morning, when I had a bit of work to catch up on and decided that the office was the best place to do it.

There was an air of Sunday about the morning as a whole. A complete reversal of the weekday role.

The further reaches of the town-the more upmarket residential parts-where peace and quiet could be guaranteed during the week, were hives of activity as paper boys delivered later than usual, and cars received their ritual weekly pampering, to the background chatter of mowers paying dutiful attention to their manicured green swards. While the town centre, alive and bustling with activity during the week, was like a ghost town.

I let myself into the office, and made my way to the cheerless, cold reporters' room.

I looked out across the equally cheerless, cold canal, towards the Hope Street Methodist Church, which within the hour would become one of the focal points of Greybridge spiritual life.

An involuntary shiver went through my body.

I remembered that the editor had an electric fire in his office. I picked up my typewriter and made my way through. If I didn't do anything drastic, like rearrange the paper clips, no one would be any the wiser. But I certainly would be a sight more comfortable. I switched on the electric fire, and stood for a moment looking through the window into Victoria Street.

Between the Victoria Street Mixed Infants playground and the pavement was a low wall. It had been topped originally with iron railings, which had long since disappeared, shorn away to help the war effort.

The street was more or less deserted, apart from three elderly men, all seated together on a bench placed by the low wall fronting the old school.

They were all dressed in their Sunday best. Jackets with collarless shirts. Two of them wore caps, one was bare-headed.

It was obvious from their appearance that they were long past retiring age, and had in all probability from their appearance spent most of their working life at Greybridge's now defunct colliery, or one of the heavy engineering works on the far side of town.

They reminded me initially of the three wise monkeys. Except that these three appeared to stare straight ahead seeing nothing. If they heard anything, they showed no visible signs. And they appeared to say very little either.

They just sat there.

If these were the people Walter Piggin saw as having the destiny of the *Pioneer* in their hands, heaven help us!

*   *   *   *

I found a couple of hours on a Sunday morning could save me best part

of a day during the week, and as I had little else to do before opening time, my Sunday trips to the office became a regular feature of the working week.

And every week, unless it was bucketing down, the three elderly men would be sitting on the wall, always dressed the same. Always seated in the same positions.

The first time I spoke to them, I thought perhaps they were hard of hearing. I had to walk past them on my way to the Mitre, so I offered a cheery "Good morning."

There was no reply. Not a flicker that they were even aware of me.

I paused and looked back before heading for the lounge bar.

"Morning," grunted the one nearest, who I later learned was Eddie, without moving his head, and almost without moving his lips.

This ritual went on every time I passed them. When I came out of the Mitre half an hour later, they had gone.

I mentioned them to the landlord, who knew very little about them, except that they came from 'somewhere down Crimea Street way', had been sitting on that wall every Sunday morning for as long as he could remember, and hadn't spent so much as a brass farthing over his bar. Thus ended the conversation.

The Sunday morning ritual for the three wise monkeys was the same every week.

First one would arrive and sit down. Then a second. Then a third.

Never a word appeared to be spoken between them.

Every time I looked out of the window, they appeared to be sitting in silence, motionless, staring straight ahead, obviously quite content just to share each other's company. They were as much a fixture as the old wooden bench on which they sat.

Until one Sunday morning, as the bright colours of summer began to give way to the deceptively warm-looking browns and golds of autumn, when I arrived at the office to find that Eddie was not there.

The three wise monkeys had become two.

Throughout the morning, I kept a vigilant eye on them, expecting Eddie to turn up at any minute.

But he didn't.

When I had finished, I went down to find out what had happened to him.

"Morning," I said as I approached the two men.

There was no reply. They stared straight ahead, dour as ever.

"Look, I..."

"Morning," came the reply before I could go on.

"Er... I couldn't help wondering where your friend was this morning," I asked.

Still no indication that they had heard me, seen me, or indeed cared.

But this time I felt they would get round to answering me in their own good time.

"Eddie," mumbled the battered cap.

I decided to direct my attention to him. He was obviously the spokesman of the duo.

"The one who sits at this end," I said in a bid to clarify the situation.

I waited.

"Eddie," came the reply.

This time from the man without the headgear.

At least they appeared to be unanimous. It was Eddie.

"I was wondering," I went on. "Well, if he's all right. I hope he's not ill or anything."

I directed this at the one who had last spoken.

There was silence for best part of a minute, though it seemed more like ten.

"He's not ill," droned the cap.

His expression becoming even more grim, if that was possible.

"I'm very glad to hear it," I replied. "You three have become quite a fixture round here on a Sunday morning."

"Gone."

"Sorry?" I said. "I'm not with you."

"Eddie's gone, 'asn't he. He's not ill. He's gone."

He fished in his pocket and pulled out a battered old pipe. He started to tap it out on the wall.

That was obviously the end of the conversation. My presence was superfluous.

I decided to leave the two alone with their memories.

I remembered Walter Piggin's little pep talk to me.

"It's people who count. It's people our readers want to know about."

"Human interest stories are the lifeblood of weekly newspapers."

Instead of going into the Mitre, I went back to the office to pick up one of the standard obituary forms we used for anyone whose demise was worth more than a paid for entry in the Births, Marriages and Deaths column.

I hurried back down to Victoria Street. The two men were still there, alone with their thoughts. Neither of them looked up as I approached.

"I wonder if you could tell me a bit about your friend Eddie," I asked.

I waited for the expected silence to run its course.

"What do you want to know for?" inquired the hatless one.

"I'm from the paper," I told him. "The *Pioneer*. I thought we might put a small piece in next week about Eddie. He's obviously been around these parts a long time. I think our readers will be interested."

The silence this time was not so prolonged.

"Oh, aye," said battered cap, half-statement, half query.

Whether it related to his acceptance that I was from the paper, that Eddie had been round these parts a long time or that our readers would be interested in him was not clear.

What was clear was that we did still have a line of communication open.

"Perhaps you could tell me his name," I asked.

The more rotund of the two men turned to face me for the first time. His skin was pock-marked with black dust, his alert, pale blue eyes boring through me like gimlets.

"Eddie," he said, through the wheeziness that many colliery workers finished their working life with, if they were indeed lucky enough to reach retirement.

"Eddie who?" I asked gently. With anyone else, my patience would have been paper thin by now.

But with this pair it was impossible not to take things at their pace.

"Eddie Fenton," volunteered his mate.

"And his address?" I asked.

The two men glanced at each other.

"Crimea Street," flat cap replied.

"Twenty-two."

"You've obviously known him a long time."

"Do you know what he did?" I went on.

Flat cap was the first to take it up.

"Did?" he wheezed. "When?"

"What was his job?"

"Ought to," he replied. "Seeing as I worked with him for nigh on forty years."

"Down the pit?" I volunteered.

He looked at me again, the face weary and worn, but the eyes as bright and alert as a hawk's.

"That's right," he said. He didn't ask how I came to that conclusion.

From then on it became progressively easier. The two men, having decided that I was a member of the human race and more or less harmless, were quite co-operative. In fact towards the end, they seemed to be trying to outdo each other, to see who could come up with the answer first, to try to top each other's stories with one of their own. By the time I had finished, I had enough material on the departed Eddie Fenton to fill best part of a page.

I thanked them both, and invited them for a pint in the Mitre for their trouble.

They declined. So I went for a quick half myself. When I came back, they had gone.

*   *   *   *

The following day, I got down to writing my piece on Eddie Fenton. The editor wanted local colour. He was certainly going to get it. There was no chance of doing justice to Eddie in that week's paper. I decided to write it up in full for the following week.

When I told the editor about the sudden departure of one of Greybridge's true sons of the earth, whose very life had reflected the changing history and fortunes of the town over best part of seventy three years, he was delighted.

"Can you fill half a page?" he asked.

"Well, I don't know if it's worth that." I said.

The editor beamed at me.

"Human interest. That's the thing that sells papers."

I did Eddie Fenton proud. Told the story of how, as the youngest of a family of nine, he was destined for the pit from the day he was born. How he was born and died in the same house in the same street that had belonged to three generations of his family before him. How he had toiled all his life to make a decent living, relentlessly fighting for better conditions so that the future sons of Greybridge would not have to go through what he did.

How he had ended his life in almost total isolation from his family, having urged them to seek greener pastures elsewhere and used what bit of money he had managed to scrape together to help them on their way.

I had turned an unknown old man sat on a bench into a folk hero.

*   *   *   *

The following Sunday morning, the brilliant sunshine added an extra sparkle to the crisp autumn air.

I was in the office bright and early.

The first job I did was check the page proof that had come in from the printer the day before.

I wandered through to the editor's office, a warm feeling of contentment that stems from a job well done welling up inside me.

I switched the fire on and crossed to the window.

I glanced down at the wall, where I knew the two men would be arriving any minute.

I wouldn't show them the page proof. I would take them copies of the paper next weekend. Show them what a wonderful tribute we had created between us to their old mate.

I went into the reporters' room and made myself a cup of coffee. On my way back to the desk in the editor's room, I glanced across the road.

I froze, the coffee halfway to my lips.

There, with his two mates, was the dear departed Eddie – as large as life!

I dropped the page proof on the table and hurried downstairs. I strode across the road to where the three men were sat in their usual place on the bench.

"I thought you said he'd gone," I bawled as I approached.

The three men stared in front of them.

"Morning," said Eddie.

"Good morning," I replied impatiently.

Flat cap looked up at me, the trace of a smile coming from his pale blue eyes.

"This is the feller we were telling you about, Eddie," he wheezed.

"I thought you were dead," I stammered.

There was no pause this time.

"Dead!" yelled Eddie, as though he'd been stung.

"Do I look dead?"

"No, of course you don't. It was your friends here."

"We didn't say he were dead."

"You said he'd gone," I countered.

Flat cap gave a wheezing chuckle that became a cough.

"That's right. Gone to his sister's," he spluttered.

"Mind you," said Eddie. "For all I get up to there, I might as well be dead!"

* * * *

I went back to the office and hurriedly went through the council minutes to see if there was anything at all I could dig out to fill the gaping hole that the non-demise of Eddie Fenton had left us with.

I managed to dredge up a plan for proposed changes to the shopping precinct that had been brought up at least three times in the last six months, and promptly dispatched again.

There wasn't a snowball in hell's chance of it getting off the ground this century. But the page had to be filled with something.

I decided not to say anything to W.C. The crunch would come soon enough. I'd face the music when I had to and not until then.

The call came from the editor's office just before lunch on Wednesday.

I knocked on the door frame.

"Come in," urged the agitated voice.

I went in, but he was nowhere to be seen.

"Hello" I called.

"I've dropped my blasted rubber again," came the editor's voice from under his desk.

He hauled himself to his feet.

"I suppose it'll turn up."

"And what can I do for you?"

"You wanted to see me," I replied stoically.

If I was going to get a rollocking, I would at least bear it with dignity.

"I suppose it's about losing the Eddie Fenton piece."

"That's right," said the editor.

"Inspired bit of thinking that."

"Inspired?" I couldn't hide my surprise.

"Putting that plan for the precinct in its place," said Walter, with a broad smile.

"It isn't new," I confessed.

"But it's controversial," beamed the editor.

"Gets people talking. Makes them sit up and take notice."

"Now *that's* the stuff that sells papers. *Controversy!*"

6

THE editor's promise that the one thing the *Pioneer* was not short of was opportunity came home to me in a very short time. This was due in no small part to the feud that had been going on between Elliot Forbes and Walter Charlesworth Piggin for some 40 years.

The pair had been at school together, where they had been the best of friends. Both had wanted to be journalists as long ago as that. But when they left school, their careers, initially at least, had taken different directions.

Walter had managed to get a job as office boy at the *Pioneer,* which turned out to be a great disappointment to his parents. Walter Piggin senior was a highly respected figure in the town, assistant manager of the Market Street branch of the National Provincial Bank, and he had a finger in most of the pies that spelled respectability in pre-war Britain. It was naturally assumed that young Walter, with a not inconsiderable academic record at school, would follow his father into the profession.

But young Walter was made of sterner stuff. He knew what he wanted to do from the age of ten, had pursued his interest by first contributing to, then editing, the school's quarterly news sheet, and if starting on the road to professional journalism meant starting on the wrong end of a tea pot at the *Gazette,* as it was still known fondly in those days, then so be it.

His mother and father had eventually agreed to him taking the job on a trial basis for three months, feeling certain that well before that time, a boy of such academic ability and business promise would be bored out of his mind. They couldn't have been more wrong, of course, and apart from service in the Army pay corps during the war, Walter Charlesworth Piggin had been there ever since.

He had recorded his own marriage - to Vera Parkes, elder daughter of Lionel and Edna Parkes, proprietors of Parkes Drapery Store. He had recorded the birth of his own two children, Jeremy and Victoria, now grown up and married with children of their own. And he had dutifully recorded in words and pictures his first grand-daughter's finest hour as she was installed as Rose Queen at Hope Street Methodist Sunday School.

Over the years, Walter Charlesworth Piggin had become as much a part of Greybridge as the Town Hall clock.

And so too had Elliot Forbes, though his links with the Pioneer didn't go back so far as Walter's. Only a mere 18 years.

When he left school, his desire to be a journalist was overshadowed by his eagerness to keep Ethel Simkins in the manner to which she would like to have become accustomed.

Ethel, by all accounts, was not a particularly pretty girl, but attractive in a vulgar sort of way. She had taken it upon herself at a very early age to assume responsibility for sex education at Albert Road Central School, and there wasn't a function of the human body that Ethel couldn't graphically explain.

But as is frequently the case with such teenage sirens, there was always one boy who wouldn't have a word said against her. It was in her interests to cultivate such a relationship - if only for the sake of respectability. To keep the young, promiscuous adolescent just the right side of being a slag.

The impressionable youth was Elliot.

So when, through the good offices of his father, Elliot was offered a job at Grafton's engineering works, he jumped at it.

It was a job with prospects. A career. A proper apprenticeship. And apart from all that, his dad had promised to buy him a second hand bicycle to get to work on - which would also come in very handy for his frequent trips to the back entry that ran behind Ethel Simkins' house.

The relationship didn't last, of course.

Ethel Simkins was married very young to a visiting curate, left Greybridge and was never heard of again.

Elliot Forbes, meanwhile, was not too distressed by this time. He was left with an apprenticeship, a second-hand bicycle and a few shillings in his pocket of a Saturday night to buy a few ales with the lads.

When the war came, being in the occupation he was, Elliot was considered of more use in the engineering works - which was by now working flat out on munitions - than in the armed forces. So there he stayed.

But at the end of the war, when the more fortunate of his contemporaries were back in town with their tales of life beyond Greybridge, Elliot started to think maybe there was life beyond Grafton's production line.

By this time, his life-long friend Walter Piggin was a reporter with the *Gazette,* and seemingly doing very nicely thank you. Elliot's thoughts started to drift back to his first love - journalism.

So when Grafton's decided to start up a staff magazine, Elliot took the first step to fame and fortune by talking his way into the job of editorial assistant.

Two years later, he got his first job on the *Pioneer,* considerably junior to Walter, who was now married with Jeremy well on the way.

Elliot was married by now, but with Jennifer, his wife, well on the way, too - out of his life!

Both men, in their different ways, were content with their lot.

Walter, plodding slowly, ponderously, but ever forward. Elliot spluttering along in fits and starts. Although there had been several women in his life, he had never married again. Some three years after joining the paper, he came to the conclusion that his talents were wasted there, and he moved away to take up a similar job on a neighbouring paper.

Within two years, he was back.

He stayed this time, until the *Herald* group made a big push to mop up the weekly newspaper readership in Greybridge, to supplement its successful evening paper operation.

Elliot found himself with a job across town in a go-ahead, dynamic operation where he could have gone right to the top if he'd had it in him. He was back at the *Pioneer* with six months.

Hard work, responsibility and Elliot Forbes didn't lie happily together. And he had been with the *Pioneer* ever since.

Elliot's constant complaint was that with his superior experience - he had worked on three newspapers to Walter's one - it was he who should by rights be occupying Walter's chair. But if anyone had even looked like offering him such an exalted position, he would have turned tail and ran.

He was one of life's eternal right-hand men, was Elliot Forbes, and no one was more aware of it than he was.

No one could deny that younger people such as Dawn, Gary, and now myself, would come and go as long as the Greybridge and District Pioneer Group of Newspapers existed, but it was unthinkable that the group would ever be the same without the likes of W.C. and Elliot Forbes.

To many folk, they *were* the *Pioneer*. And quite rightly so.

Walter and Elliot were the hierarchy. The elder statesmen.

Walter did most of the page planning himself. He had his own contacts for stories. People who had come to know him and trust him over the years. He wrote the editorial comment every week - the voice of Greybridge. While Elliot busied himself working the Town Hall beat - where his opinions were frequently more respected than those of the councillors who were elected to voice them - and making the odd sortie to the police station to share the occasional cup of cocoa with Inspector Crabtree, who I would have sworn was older than Adam's dog.

The two younger reporters had their own sections of town life to cover. Which left me in a bit of a pig-in-the-middle situation.

It seemed that Walter's definition of opportunity, of experience in all aspects of journalism, when he took me on was that I mopped up in all those areas that he and Elliot didn't wish to, and Dawn and Gary weren't designated to.

Not that I minded too much. Variety did indeed prove to be the spice of weekly newspaper life, and I rapidly found myself in a sort of no man's land between Elliot and W.C. on the one hand and Gary and Dawn on the other.

I knew I had no official authority vested in me to do so, but increasingly I found myself having to direct operations in the reporter's room, simply because if I hadn't, no one else would.

Dawn was no problem. She went about her work happily and cheerfully, a pleasure to have around. On the occasional nights I did get lumbered with a job I could well have done without, she wouldn't hesitate to volunteer to step in, even if it meant dragging her hapless boyfriend along with her because she'd already agreed to see him that night.

She had seen her share of hardship, had Dawn. Her father had died in tragic circumstances when she was only 12. As she was an only child, much responsibility had fallen on her shoulders to carry her mother through the emotional and practical difficulties following her father's death. She had experienced very little of a normal teenage adolescence. She had to grow up from childhood to adulthood virtually overnight. And she had coped admirably.

As for Gary, he was something else entirely.

An only child, he had received the best education that money could buy from the age of three.

His father was a director of one of the biggest textile mills in Lancashire.

His mother was a pillar of the local W.I. and an expert on country crafts.

They had both resolved that any children of theirs would not go short of anything. It was fortunate for Gary that they only had the one child to reap the benefits of all their self-sacrifice. And if the only thanks they sought was to see their only son take full advantage of the privileges they had put his way, there was no way Gary was going to disappoint them.

Unfortunately, Gary felt the same way about much of the rest of the world.

Life was a game to him. He would sit and argue, debate a point for hours, in a bid to justify his not doing something or other, knowing full well that it would have taken but half the time to do the job in the first place. But that wasn't the point. Gary had to win.

That's when he was actually in the office. Because it obviously hadn't taken him long to realise that the more time he spent away from the place, the less likely he was to get landed with something he didn't want to do and couldn't wriggle out of.

The regular calls that are common to any journalist were manna from heaven to Gary.

Every Monday morning, the local clergy would be contacted for a list or events that were coming up that week, and any odd snippets of local chat from the weekend.

Secretaries of local organisations would be contacted at regular intervals - and in a close-knit community like Greybridge, this was no small task.

And every morning, the local police and fire stations were given a call to see if anything dramatic had happened overnight - in our terms, a vagrant found asleep on the steps of the War Memorial was dramatic if there was little else happening that day.

Elliot made the regular police and fire calls. Dawn did most of the organisations run by the women of the borough. While Gary did the churches and anything else that came under the general banner of lifeblood of a weekly newspaper.

Most of these calls could be done by telephone. But to Gary, every one had to be a personal visit.

"You don't get involved with the community sat on your backside in an office," he said.

"It's important to keep up the personal contact."

It certainly was in his case. Anything to get away from the office.

A press conference that amounted to little more than a free drink and a snack; a photo call where a caption would suffice and which was well within the scope of the photographer to collect - they were all meat and drink to Gary.

But for him, the icing on the cake was the long, despairing wail of the siren that heralded the call-out of the fire brigade.

When Gary was in the office, his hand was a blur as it shot to the phone.

"*Pioneer*. Where's the call?"

The duty officer would tell him.

"Thanks. See you."

A man of few words in a situation like this, was Gary. He was on his way. Through the door like a rat up a drainpipe. Any requests from me or Elliot as to where he was going fell on deaf ears. Within seconds, the engine of his well-worn MG roared into life and he was on his way. Gone.

True, there may have been a dramatic story to follow up. And if one of our reporters could be first on the scene, they could not only get a good first-hand story for the *Pioneer,* but perhaps collect the odd pound or two by phoning the story through to the daily papers.

But the truth of the matter was that in Greybridge and district the vast majority of calls for the fire brigade were to chip pan fires, cats stuck up trees, cars mysteriously bursting into flames, flooded kitchens during the cold snap, and the occasional child's head stuck in a pan. Very little, in fact, that couldn't have been picked up on the routine telephone call the following morning.

But to Gary, it was a heaven-sent opportunity for him to see the office in the light he liked best - through his rear view mirror as he raced away!

Every time he took off at the speed of light on what I was sure was going to be another abortive outing, I couldn't resist a silent prayer, fervently hoping that if neither I, nor Elliot, nor W.C. could get him to see the error of his ways, the good Lord himself may intervene on our behalf to do something to even up the score.

Our faith was not misplaced!

When it did happen, it came in a most unexpected and incredibly satisfying way to those who were privileged to witness it.

* * * *

About a week or so before Christmas, it was traditional for the management to foot the bill for a meal for the staff - an occasion graced by no less a mortal than our revered proprietor himself, Aubrey Dalrymple Hogg, who always managed to succeed in convincing everyone present how little he knew about newspapers, what a silly great puddock he was, and how fortunate we were not to see more of him.

It was usual to start the proceedings with a drink at the Mitre straight after work, and go on to the meal from there.

Gary was late back from lunch. About an hour late. Dawn and I were up to our eyes trying to clear a backlog of work.

"Nice of you to show up," I greeted him sarcastically without looking up as he strolled casually into the room.

"It's gratifying to know you can still find your way back to the office."

"What do you mean?" asked Gary with an air of innocence.

"You're very lucky we're still here," I replied, "They could have put a motorway through here, the time you've been away."

Gary was totally unruffled.

"If you'd look inside that diary you guard so carefully these days," he said casually, "you'd see there was a presentation at the junior school. I just happened to look in, didn't I?"

"Well now you are here," I started.

48

For the first time since Gary came in, I looked up from what I was doing. If Gary had called in at the presentation, he hadn't been there above seconds. It must have taken him best part of two hours to get ready.

He was wearing an off-white lightweight suit, black shirt open to the navel, exposing a gold medallion heavy enough to make him round-shouldered for life.

"Fancy dress, was it?" I asked coolly.

"What do you mean?" queried Gary - a phrase that had by now become his trademark.

"You could hardly expect me to go and meet the proprietor dressed like..."

He looked me up and down pointedly.

"Dressed like what?" I pressed.

He thought better of coming out with the obvious reply.

"Are you going to discuss my sartorial elegance all afternoon? Or do you want me to actually work for a living?" he ventured.

"Funny you should ask," I said, handing over the minutes of the Road Safety Committee.

"There are at least a dozen paragraphs to be got out of that lot. You've got an hour."

Gary reluctantly took the minutes and looked at them none too enthusiastically, as Dawn came into the office.

She stopped short when she saw Greybridge's answer to Action Man.

"Don't say a word," I warned. Gary was itching for someone to open up the conversation again. He beamed in Dawn's direction, generating enough warmth to make toast.

She ignored him and turned to me.

"What about?" she asked.

I smiled as she walked across to her desk, leaving Gary silently fuming.

"And if that phone rings in the next hour, I answer it," I announced.

No reply.

"Understood?"

Dawn nodded. Gary turned a deaf ear.

And with that, I picked up the copy I had prepared for the editor's attention and took it through to his office.

* * * *

I heard the low wail of the fire siren start up then swell to a crescendo before I reached the editor's desk.

I dropped the copy into his tray, turned and sprinted back. But I was too late.

Gary was already on the phone.

"Cheers," he said. "See you."

He slammed the phone down and sprang to his feet.

"Now hang on a minute," I said, trying to block his path.

His six feet tall, 14-stone frame swept past me as if I wasn't there.

"Can't stop," he called. "This could be the big one."

"What? Where?" I yelled after him as he legged it down the stairs.

"See you," came the reply. And the front door crashed closed behind him.

"What have I got to do?" I moaned. "Chain him to the flaming desk?"

Dawn smiled sympathetically.

Just then the phone rang. Dawn looked across at me.

"You get it," I said.

I went back to my own desk, as Dawn picked up the phone.

"*Pioneer*".

She listened for a minute, then covered the mouthpiece.

"It's for Elliot," she said. "Inspector Crabtree."

I took the phone.

"Hello, Inspector. I'm afraid Elliot's out at the moment. Can I help?"

I listened with interest.

"Thanks a lot, Inspector. See you."

I replaced the phone.

"So that's where gorgeous Gary's gone."

Dawn was watching me with interest.

"That fire siren," I said. "There's been a report that somebody's fallen in the river. By Pitter's Bridge."

*   *   *   *

The Meadows was a well-used beauty spot on the south side of Greybridge, cutting off the hustle and bustle of the town from the homes of the better-heeled residents of the borough.

It had at one time been just grazing land, but the local authority, ever-vigilant to the need for improved leisure facilities, had made the most of it over the years. There was now a considerable amount of woodland, laced with signed walkways, drawing attention to the flora that abounded there. At the bottom of the valley flowed the river, which at one time had served the old flour mill.

We headed along the top road and dropped down to where Pitter's Bridge crossed the river, swollen by the recent rain.

As we approached the bridge, we could see the activity. There were two fire engines drawn up in the field as near to the river as was safe, bearing in mind the slippery condition of the bank.

An ambulance was pulled up on the car park next to a police panda car, where a young constable was talking to the ambulance men.

I pulled in by the side of them. There was a lot of activity by the river bank as firemen, up to their thighs in the muddy, chilling water, grappled with some unidentified object.

Blocking my view, keeping a safe distance from the action, was Gary, standing out like a beacon in his near-white suit.

"What happened?" I asked the constable hurriedly.

He shrugged. "He must have slipped down the bank."

"Is he all right?" asked Dawn.

"He will be. Once he gets back on dry land. Had a bit of a soaking. But I can't see him coming to much harm."

I tried to get a clearer view of what was happening, but Gary still blocked my view. The firemen seemed to have quite a struggle on their hands.

One of the ambulancemen slammed the back doors of his vehicle.

"Right. We'll be off," he called.

"I'll see you," replied the policeman. "Sorry you've had a wasted journey."

"Aren't you going to take him to hospital?" Dawn inquired in some surprise. "I would have thought at least a check-up..."

"Sorry, love. But there's no way we can get him in there."

"They were never built for horses!"

"Horses? That's a horse?"

"That's right," he smiled. "Must have gone too near the edge. Slipped down the bank."

We looked across again at the struggling scene by the river, which we could now see more clearly. It was indeed a horse. One-time bay, but now covered in mud.

The firemen had a couple of hoses round it and were taking the strain as the horse tried to get sufficient footing to scramble up the bank.

"Come on," yelled one of the firemen. "Don't just stand there."

Gary looked round to see who he was talking to.

"You, you clown."

Gary gingerly grabbed hold of the loose end of the hose trailing behind the rear fireman, as everyone put in a concerted effort to drag the hapless animal clear.

"I'll go and give them a hand," I said to Dawn.

"You stay here."

But I didn't have to.

Suddenly, the horse clambered up the bank, and was free. Gary let out a plaintive yell as he fell backwards with three firemen crashing down on top of him.

The horse whinnied and trotted off to higher, safer ground. Dawn and I looked at each other, desperately trying not to smile.

We both failed miserably.

Gary got slowly to his feet, his off-white suit plastered with thick mud.

"Nice one, Gary mate," I called.

"We're proud of you."

For the first time since we arrived, he became aware of our presence. He opened his mouth, but no words came out.

"You were right, weren't you," I called. "You don't get involved in the community sat on your backside in the office."

I headed back to the car.

Dawn followed me.

"I'm glad he didn't hurt himself," she said as we got in.

"I suppose so," I conceded. "I know he's a a bit of a pain at times, but I wouldn't wish him any harm."

"I didn't mean Gary," she smiled.

"I meant the horse!"

7

"THERE'S nothing goes on in this town that I don't know about," thundered Elliot Forbes across the top of a pint pot in a quiet corner of the Mitre.

"Nothing!"

At least, it had been a quiet corner until I had touched on a raw nerve.

I was trying to pay him a compliment. I only happened to remark on the fact that he seemed to dig up the most amazing stories without ever moving from his desk.

But Elliot, with a couple of pints of Branson's best bitter under his belt, immediately jumped to the defensive.

"I know you and the kids run round like blue-arsed flies for your bits of weekly tittle-tattle, but who gets the real stories in this paper?"

It invited a response. I was desperately searching the depths of my brain to give him one that wouldn't upset him.

I needn't have bothered.

"I do. And the lad in the front office."

The lad in the front office being Walter Charlesworth Piggin.

"And do you know why?" he went on.

Again I probed the inner reaches of my mind for the right answer.

"I'll tell you," he went on. "Respect. Trust. And that's not something you pick up in a college classroom."

"That's something that has to be worked for. Earned."

"And you don't do that in five minutes, I can tell you."

He could. And he had done. On more than one occasion.

In fact, whenever we got into one of these end of the day drinking sessions, the conversation always turned this way.

Because in spite of his long experience, his privileged position on the *Pioneer* - where he had a secure job without ever needing to break into a sweat until he qualified for his bus pass - Elliot Forbes was basically an insecure man.

He needed constant reassurance that he was a success in his own little world. Someone of importance. Someone to be looked up to. And it was to me he turned for it more often than not.

Not because he respected me more than the others, though I liked to flatter myself that perhaps he did.

But because I always seemed to be the one to end up at this corner table sharing his company at the end of the working day.

"You see, lad," he put a massive paw on my shoulder.

"Experience is the name of the game in this business."

"You've got to get to know people. Let them see they can trust you. Become part of their lives. Gain their confidence."

He leaned closer as if to emphasise the point.

I momentarily reflected on how less appealing the fragrance of Branson's best bitter was second hand.

"When you've done that, you don't have to go looking for stories. They come to you."

He sat back, pondered his pint pot, then lifted it slowly to his lips. Point made.

"You're right," I said. "There's no substitute for experience. And with the years you've got tucked under your belt..."

"All right. So I know I'm an ancient bugger."

I didn't seem to be able to say a right word.

"I didn't say that," I offered quickly.

"Well I am," agreed Elliot.

"But I've still got my finger on the pulse of this town, believe me."

That wasn't quite where Elliot had his finger according to Gary, but in the interests of bringing the session to a speedy close, I agreed with him. Wholeheartedly.

I drank up.

"Well," I said, trying to sound as casual as I could.

"Time I wasn't here."

"You've got time for another," thundered the amiable bearded giant, snapping out from under his cloud of moroseness.

"Some other time," I said. "I really should be off."

"Alec. Same again when you're ready," bawled Elliot across to the bar.

Alec moved to the pumps.

There was no point arguing.

"Just the one," I conceded. "Then I really must be off," knowing full well that if I didn't play my cards very carefully I would still be sitting there saying the same thing in two hours time.

I couldn't help but marvel at how nature had managed to put together such a creature as Elliot Forbes. A man who could appear as dormant as a hibernating dormouse during office hours and suddenly come to life at opening time.

If Elliot Forbes hadn't been born, Branson's Brewery would have had to invent him.

*　　*　　*　　*

He was right, of course. Years of working, living, breathing the life of Greybridge had made Elliot Forbes and Walter Piggin legends in the town.

You only had to walk down the street with either of them to realise that.

I swear there wasn't a man, woman or child in the town who didn't know them, who wouldn't stop to pass the time of day.

And it was true they did have the confidence of everyone who mattered and their connections frequently made the difference between a superficial story and a gutsy piece of informed local journalism.

But not everything comes to he who waits in the world of weekly newspapers. Not even to Elliot Forbes.

To get him to accept this was something else.

But one day. One day…

*　　*　　*　　*

Elliot Forbes didn't have many close friends outside his newspaper contacts.

In fact, he didn't have much life at all outside the *Pioneer*. His cronies were drawn from the ranks of those who had matured in the town alongside Elliot and who were of his vintage.

Such a man was Inspector Maurice Makepeace Crabtree, who had lorded it over Greybridge Police Station for many years.

The two men had a considerable amount in common. Both viewed the world with a heavy cynicism - a world which seemed to start and end with the borough boundaries.

Both felt they were fighting an uphill battle against a tide of permissiveness that was threatening to sweep away all the old standards and values.

And both felt that their efforts to make the world a better place to live in were grossly undervalued by the powers that be.

The one time you could reckon on it being safe to go into the Mitre for a quiet drink without being accosted by Elliot Forbes was when he was in the company of Maurice Makepeace Crabtree.

They acted as a catalyst for each other's self pity, rapidly becoming totally unaware of the existence of anybody else.

At the root of their relationship was the mutual recognition of a soulmate.

And it was true that whenever there was anything happening locally that would be of the remotest interest to the *Pioneer,* the Inspector would make sure that Elliot was the first to know.

Living proof, in Elliot's eyes, that he really did have his finger on the pulse at all times.

*   *   *   *

Greybridge Police Station stood in the centre of the town, just off the market square, a permanent monument to architectural bad taste.

Its only redeeming feature was the clock that crowned its red-tiled roof, which had the distinction of being the only public clock in Greybridge that was going and right, within ten minutes either way.

Adjoining the police station, like a dilapidated site office, was the building that served as the magistrates' court, where the worthy local justices sat every Thursday morning in judgment on their fellow men of less integrity and social responsibility than they.

Each morning, at ten o'clock sharp, the local press would turn up at Greybridge Police Station to be briefed on the criminal activity of the past 24 hours.

Break-in at Meadowside Drive. Domestic on Cork Street. Indecent exposure in the cemetery.

By and large, they were a fairly orderly bunch in Greybridge.

Occasionally we did have the big case, which had been duly recorded for posterity in the annals of the town.

The notorious draper who had battered his wife to death - no relation, I hasten to add, to Walter Piggin's esteemed in-laws. The armed robbery at the old Trustee Savings Bank premises, long since converted to a snooker hall.

But anyone in this league merely put in a brief appearance to be remanded to some higher court of justice, while the magistrates were left to plod through their weekly roll-call of petty misdemeanours.

There was usually enough on the court sheet on a Thursday to see them comfortably through until lunchtime.

Occasionally, the hearings went on until four o'clock in the afternoon, usually following Christmas and New Year, or any other period of jollity and merrymaking, when Greybridge seemed to have more than its share of vigorous felons who felt it compulsory to carry things to excess.

Each morning, Elliot Forbes would put in an appearance at the police station sharp on the stroke of ten o'clock.

As the desk sergeant opened the book and read out anything of interest, Elliot would watch the proceedings with a disinterested air, noting only the odd address, or name that needed spelling out, while committing the rest to memory.

Within ten minutes, the ritual was complete. The reporters took their leave and went about the rest of their business. But not Elliot.

"Is he in yet?" he would inquire of the desk sergeant, with a nod towards the back of the station.

The desk sergeant would silently lift the flap that separated the public at large from intimate contact with law and order.

Elliot would follow him along a dark, Victorian corridor to the end. The sergeant would rap on the sturdy oak door, wait for the gruff "Come in" from the other side, then, without a word, walk away, leaving Elliot to make his own entrance into the private world of Maurice Makepeace Crabtree, Inspector in Her Majesty's Constabulary.

The two men would share each other's company for maybe half an hour over a cup of cocoa.

Then Elliot would take his leave, while the Inspector got on with the more pressing tasks of the day.

This was the routine on most days. Most days, that is, except Thursdays.

On Thursday mornings, Elliot would propel his huge frame through the portals of the court house and take up position on the front row of the press bench, just behind the legal representatives and prosecuting police officer - his close friend and ally, Inspector Crabtree.

So with Elliot firmly esconced in Greybridge Magistrates Court, the task of making the police call on Thursday mornings invariably fell to me.

After one such call, I hung around after the other lads had left to have a quick work with Sergeant Jim Blacker, who played badminton with one or two of us most Wednesday nights.

We were trying to get a bit of a league going, and Jim had been trying to whip up a bit of enthusiasm among his colleagues.

"Hang on a minute," he called.

He turned to a young constable who was picking out a report with one finger on a typewriter that looked as if it had belonged to Noah.

"What time are those two jokers on?"

Constable Wade stopped typing.

"Bill and Ben? Not likely before half ten. They'll give us a shout."

Jim glanced at his watch.

"Better make sure they're ready. We don't want one of them keeping the magistrates waiting while he goes to the bog."

"Right, Sarge."

With a final prod with his index finger, he got up and dutifully went to see to the needs of Bill and Ben.

Bill and Ben were two brothers, itinerant second-hand dealers who were almost as well-known to the local magistrates as the police. They lived on the outskirts of town in an old caravan, scratching a living by collecting whatever the more affluent folk of Greybridge were pleased to be rid of, and re-selling most of their wares in the local market every Tuesday and Friday, having come to an arrangement with a stallholder to rent part of his pitch for a fiver a day.

Most of the proceeds could be guaranteed to pass across the bar of the Victoria Arms, and quite frequently the brothers would end up occupying a police cell for the night.

It could be a long haul back to the caravan on a wet and windy winter's night, and it was never beyond the wit of the two men to engineer enough of a fracas to bring the police in. Not that they were violent men. They weren't. But they were big and intimidating - particularly in an argument.

"What are they in for this time?" I asked, as Jim turned his attention back to me.

"Usual," replied Jim. "Drunk and disorderly. Causing an affray."

"So how many do you reckon we need?"

He had dismissed Bill and Ben from his thoughts and turned his attention to more pressing matters. The badminton league.

"If you can get half a dozen," I said.

"I've got four definite," replied Jim. "Ted Houldsworth and Andy Wainwright are possibles. I can't guarantee they'll be able to play every week, though. Somebody's got to mind the shop."

I was about to suggest that on a couple of nights a week there would be no problem. They could leave Bill and Ben in charge. They probably knew the workings of Greybridge Police Station as well as anyone, the time they spent there, when Constable Wade came in from the back as if his shirt tail was on fire.

"They've gone, Sarge!" he gasped.

"Gone?" Jim looked incredulous. "They can't have gone."

"They have. I'm telling you. Cell door's open and they've scarpered."

"That's all I need," muttered Jim.

"When were they last seen?"

The young constable reported that he had come on duty at eight o'clock, and his predecessor had taken them tea in their cell.

Jim raced through to the back of the station, to the corridor where the cells were.

I followed him.

"Which one were they in?" he asked.

"Second from the end," answered the constable dutifully.

Sure enough, the door was open, the blankets were folded neatly on the bed. But there was no sign of Bill or Ben.

Jim headed back to the front office and moved swiftly into action.

"Put out a general call. I want those two picked up. And quick. If I have to go before the magistrates and tell them we've lost two prisoners, there'll be hell to pay."

The call was put out.

Then Jim had a thought.

"How did they get out?" he asked the constable, who was beginning to quite enjoy himself.

"Through the door," he said brightly.

"I know that. How? I don't suppose they had a key."

Constable Wade thought about this for a moment.

"The door mustn't have been locked," he said eventually.

There was no sign of any forcing.

"Wasn't locked!"

I thought for a moment that Jim was going to explode.

"They've never tried to do a runner before," volunteered the constable.

"This is a police station, lad," Jim thundered. "Not a holiday camp."

He glanced at his watch.

"I suppose all we can do is sit back and wait," offered the constable, trying to take the heat out of the situation.

"Is it hell as like," snorted Jim.

"Take the car. Go and have a scout round yourself."

"Check their caravan. Then have a check round the cafes."

"Particularly those near the market."

"Anywhere they use. Got it?"

"Yes, Sarge." Constable Wade took his hat from the table and disappeared into the back of the police station.

"Call themselves flaming coppers," muttered Jim.

"Have you got their full names?" I asked casually.

"Full names?"

"I only know them as Bill and Ben," I said.

Jim suddenly latched onto my train of thought.

"Oh, no. You wouldn't."

"I'm sorry, Jim. But two escaped prisoners. Half the police in the county alerted. It's too good a story to miss, isn't it?" I grinned.

I didn't catch his reply. He delivered it through clenched teeth.

The door opened and Constable Frank Ormiston poked his head round. He was on duty in the magistrates court.

"Ten minutes," he said. "You'd better be getting them up."

He disappeared again.

"Oh, my God," said Jim. "What am I going to tell them?"

"The truth?" I volunteered.

It didn't help.

Jim was beginning to realise how the Christians felt before they went to the lions.

He lifted the flap and headed for the door.

He never got there.

The door to the back of the station opened.

"Is there any chance of another cup of tea?" came a gravel voice from behind us.

Jim turned, his mouth wide open, as Ben emerged from the corridor.

"You!"

Ben looked round lazily.

"Who were you expecting?" he asked in his slow county drawl.

"Where the hell have you been?" spluttered Jim.

"With my brother. Where else would I be going?" he replied with simple logic.

"But your cell. It was empty," said Jim.

Ben beamed down from his giant frame at the bemused police sergeant.

"You didn't expect us to stay in there did you? Not with the light gone. It's bad enough having to play cards with that cheating conniving brother of mine in broad daylight without that."

"So where have you been?" asked Jim in wonderment.

"We moved in next door," said Ben candidly. "End cell. Where did you think we went. Savoy Hotel?"

"Now look, about this tea..."

Frank Ormiston stuck his head round the door again.

"Right, Jim. They're on. Sharp as you like. They're not too happy this morning."

"Hang on," Jim replied. "You can take them back with you."

He turned to Ben. "Go and get your brother. You're on."

"But we're parched," moaned Ben.

"When this lot's over, you can sup enough tea to float a battleship" said Jim, failing to hide his relief.

"I'll mash it myself."

Ben disappeared down the corridor.

"I don't believe it," muttered Jim. "I don't friggin' well believe it."

"Next friggin' cell. All the time."

Frank looked puzzled.

"Something up?" he asked.

Jim shook his head as Ben re-appeared, his brother in tow.

"Don't go away, Sarge," grinned Bill.

"We'll be right back."

We watched as the two brothers dutifully led the way out of the front door to make the short journey to face up to justice yet again.

"These young coppers," fumed Jim. "They haven't got the sense they were born with."

"How they find their way home beats me."

"I'm surprised there's anyone round here who knows what day of the week it is."

"Well I might as well be off," I said, turning to the door.

"I may see you later."

Jim grunted his reply.

"And Jim," I said, as I opened the door.

"What?" he called back.

"Don't forget to call off the chase."

"Oh, Christ," muttered the hapless Jim as he dived for the radio.

* * * *

It was mid-afternoon when I next saw Elliot Forbes.

"Good lunch?" I greeted him.

"Excellent," he said, a rosy glow warming his face, at least, the parts not engulfed by whiskers.

"Things settled down over there, then, have they?" I ventured.

"Over where?" beamed Elliot.

"The police station. After this morning's bit of excitement."

"Excitement?" repeated Elliot in disbelief.

"Nothing exciting ever happens over there."

"And if it did?" I ventured.

"I'd be the first to know, wouldn't I," replied Elliot.

"Of course," I said, stifling the smile that was welling up inside me.

"Finger on the pulse, eh?"

"Exactly," said Elliot.

"Exactly."

8

LITTLE rivulets of rain were scurrying down the outside of the grimy office window, beyond which the equally grimy, lacklustre life of Greybridge struggled to come to terms with another day, as the phone rang.

I absently picked it up as three tiny tributaries joined forces, and in a sudden rush of new-found zest, raced down the glass to the rotting wooden frame, where they were quickly swallowed up to disappear for ever.

"Greybridge Pioneer," I muttered.

"So is this," came the cheery voice from the other end. "It must be fate that's thrown us together."

"Yes, Christine," I sighed.

"One of those days, is it?"

She took my silence as confirmation.

"Well I'm sorry, lovey," she said. "But it's not going to get any better. The old man wants to see you. Good luck."

There was a click from the phone.

I replaced the receiver.

W.C.'s office adjoined the reporter's room.

All day he was in and out like a piston, without ever bothering to stand on ceremony.

But every so often he felt he had to show his authority. Live up to his role as managing editor of the *Greybridge and District Pioneer Group of Newspapers*.

On such occasions, he went through the switchboard.

He gave Christine a buzz. Gave her the name of the person he wanted to see, and got her to pass on the message.

It was a laborious way of getting his message across, and even if Christine answered the phone at the first time of bidding, which she wasn't in the habit of doing, it could still take some time. Much more time than W.C. popping his head round the door and muttering "Come in a minute."

But one thing was certain. When the call came via Christine that the editor wanted a word, it usually meant only one thing.

Trouble.

* * * *

Walter Charlesworth Piggin was seated behind his desk trying to force a plastic sandwich box into an already over-filled drawer.

He gave up the struggle, as I rapped on the door frame to announce my arrival.

"Took your time, didn't you?" he grunted.

"It must be five minutes since I called Christine."

"If it was that urgent, why didn't you come in yourself?" I was tempted to say, but thought better of it under the circumstances.

"I only just got the call," I replied dutifully.

"Was there a problem?"

The editor casually put his hand up to his mouth and brushed away a tiny flurry of digestive biscuit crumbs from his moustache with his index finger.

"I've just had a phone call," he volunteered at last.

"From Mrs Wimpenny."

He waited for the effect of this to sink in.

Mrs Wimpenny, a thin-boned, studious lady in her early fifties, with a pronounced stoop and a voice powerful enough to stop a clock, was the driving force behind Greybridge Players.

Three nights ago, I had gone along to review their current production.

A futuristic comedy set in a nuclear shelter.

This morning, my review had appeared in the paper.

I didn't need to be clairvoyant to spot the connection between these facts and her phone call.

"She is far from pleased," continued the editor.

"*Far* from pleased."

He paused for dramatic effect.

"What in Heaven's name do you think you were doing?"

"Sorry," I said. "I'm not with you."

"Not with me?" he bellowed, his colour taking on a slightly darker hue, his cheek bones becoming tinged with purple.

"You were supposed to write a *review* of the damn play."

"Not savage it like a rabid dog."

"I did write a review," I said. "It's called constructive criticism."

"And if they can't take it, they shouldn't have invited it in the first place."

I was becoming as heated as the editor.

I had given up a previously planned night out to cover the play.

I had sat through over two and half hours of what had the potential to be a reasonable dramatic work in capable hands, but in the event turned out to be as potent as cold porridge. And I had written what I considered to be a very fair piece of constructive criticism.

"It's the Greybridge Players," thundered the editor.

"Not the Royal friggin' Shakespeare Company."

"It's bank clerks, and council workers, and housewives and secretaries. Doing it in their spare time."

"And that was exactly the way it came over," I said.

"But you don't have to say it. Not in so many words."

"These people are doing their best under very trying circumstances to keep alive the theatrical tradition in Greybridge. They're to be encouraged. Not torn apart and destroyed."

"Besides, a lot of them are our advertisers."

Now we were getting to the truth of the matter. I had infringed the first rule of the freedom of the press according to the Gospel of the *Greybridge Pioneer*.

Don't upset the advertisers.

For several seconds neither of us spoke.

"Look," Walter went on at last. "I know you were doing the job to the best of your ability. And I know that most of them couldn't act their way out of a paper bag."

"But we don't have to *say* so. Not in so many words."

"What was the point in my going, then?" I asked, quite reasonably, I thought.

"Because they are part of the fabric of Greybridge," he replied.

"Because by sending someone to actually *review* the play, we make them feel important."

"And it sells papers," I added.

"Exactly," said the editor. "And after all, that's what we're here for."

I thought about this one for a second or two.

"So we just reprint the programme. Right Honourable Anthony Beamish was played by Stanley Renshaw. Mandy the maid was played by Linda Gregory."

"If you can't think of anything better to say, that's *exactly* what I mean," said the editor.

"Mention them all. If you can throw in the occasional praiseworthy adjective without rupturing your conscience, so much the better. But just remember *who* you are criticising. They may not be the National Theatre. But they are doing their best."

No one could deny that. It still didn't alter the fact that the high spot of the entire production was the interval.

"Well I think we see eye to eye on the matter," said the editor, getting to his feet. The interview was obviously over.

"What shall I do about Mrs Wimpenny?" I asked.

The editor managed a half smile.

"Don't worry about her," he said.

"I've already had a word. There are no hard feelings. Not any more."

"But next time, just watch it. All right?"

"What did you tell her?" I asked in some wonderment.

Mrs Wimpenny had the tenacity of a terrier, and the kind of disposition that could turn vinegar sour.

"The truth," replied Walter.

"I told her that the Greybridge Players had always set such high standards in this town, that we held anything they cared to produce on a par with a professional performance."

"And that is the standard by which we set our judgment."

"And that's the truth?"

"Near enough," he beamed, his eyes twinkling.

"It's what she wanted to hear."

*　　*　　*　　*

The village of Lower Greybridge (population 1,567) had been a jewel in the crown of rural England, as any resident would happily tell you, since well before Greybridge town had been even a gleam in the eye of the developers.

The only thing that had changed since the conquerors of King Harold and their successors had trod its green pastures had been the degree of affluence of the folk who chose to live there.

Before Greybridge was developed into the vigorous industrial town of the late 19th century, Lower Greybridge had been little more than a hamlet, populated in the main by farmworkers in their tied cottages or converted sub-standard buildings.

But as the town grew and became prosperous, so too did many of the people who ran it. And they wanted homes away from the grime and noise that provided their affluence. A place in the country, handy enough to get to work each day, but clean, fresh and spacious enough in which to bring up a family. Their eyes quickly settled on Lower Greybridge and the quiet revolution began, as those once unsung tied cottages and sub-standard outbuildings became prime targets for conversion.

The farmers were delighted with the sudden windfall that came from the sale of their property at hitherto undreamed of prices. And the new occupants were equally delighted to have acquired their own little stake in rural England, happy in the knowledge that all the trappings of the 20th century were no more than 15 minutes along the road.

The hub of the village community was the Victoria Hall.

Initially a disused outbuilding, it had, over the years, been developed, renovated, added-on to and modernised until it was a mixture of mock half-timbered Tudor grandeur and Victorian primness, the latter reflecting the era during which most of the reconstruction work had taken place, its name commemorating the then monarch in Lower Greybridge for evermore - or at least for as long as the Victoria Hall was standing.

But no community thrives on buildings alone. It needs people to power the treadmill of life, to generate the charge that makes village life sparkle.

And in that respect, Lower Greybridge was doubly-blessed with a twin-pronged driving force in the form of the Reverend Arnold Mycock, spiritual leader of the parish, and Miss Irene Pendlebury.

Miss Pendlebury was something of an enigma in the village. She lived in one of four mid 17th-century cottages overlooking The Green. She owned all four - and rumour had it that she owned half of the village as well, though appearances denied this. She was a tiny, well-rounded lady in her mid-50s. Her round face and rosy cheeks, matured through years in the countryside, exuded warmth and good humour. And the little knitted woollen bob hat she wore through summer and winter alike gave her the appearance of a benevolent garden gnome.

But despite her roly-poly appearance, under that tiny woollen hat perched precariously on her lank, light grey hair there was a mind as keen as mustard. Anything and everything that needed organising in Lower Greybridge found Miss Irene Pendlebury at the centre of activities.

And there was no cause dearer to her heart than the activities of the Lower Greybridge Amateur Dramatic Society.

The society put on two full-length plays a year, but was somehow involved in village life throughout the 12 months, taking part in folk festivals, staging tableaux for special occasions as and when required, as well as depicting Lower Greybridge through the ages for any carnival within a 20-mile radius of the village.

The only limitation to their activities seemed to be that their two drama productions had to fit comfortably into the confines of the Victoria Hall, and everything else on to the flat back lorry belonging to Hardy Brothers, corn and feed merchants, who willingly loaned it out for every social occasion.

I first became aware of the existence of the Lower Greybridge Amateur Dramatic Society shortly after joining the *Pioneer*. It was practically impossible not to. When they weren't actually performing, they were busy collecting funds through the whole gamut of recognised money-raising functions.

And as the members of the society in the main were also members of the village W.I., Townswomen's Guild, Parochial Church Council, school governors and community council, it was difficult to avoid mention of the dramatic society.

My first direct contact with them came some months after.

Their spring production. Not a date or time of particular significance. Except that it came right on the heels of our brush with the redoubtable Mrs Wimpenny.

And Walter Piggin left me in no doubt what was expected of me.

*   *   *   *

The Reverend Arnold Mycock had a permanently haunted expression. Standing well over six feet tall, and as slender as a hairpin, his dark clothes, gaunt features and deep-set eyes gave him the appearance of a character out of a horror film. Only his twinkling, grey eyes reflected the warmth and concern for his fellow men that exuded from within that sparse frame.

It was from him, on my weekly call to the vicarage to make a note of the following week's parish events, that I first learned of "Danby's Darkest Hour", LGADS's spring offering. Which was quite fitting, as the three-act family saga of mystery and suspense had been penned by the reverend gentleman himself.

It was the latest, and by far the most ambitious, work in his literary career, which had spanned close on 30 years, and embraced in the main short stories (one of which was actually broadcast) and nature notes for the Greybridge weekly free sheet.

"I won't tell you the plot, hmm," he said, peering at me over his brass-rimmed spectacles.

"Mustn't give anything away, hmm."

"But I can tell you there are some rattling good parts in it."

The "rattling good parts" were fairly predictable, and as he outlined them, it was a fairly easy task to mentally cast the play.

For it was apparent that one of the main reasons "Danby's Darkest Hour" had been chosen for performance was the fact that it fulfilled all the main criteria of any production considered by the LGADS.

It was three acts, which gave two intervals - one for the supply of refreshments, the other for the sale of raffle tickets in support of the church roof fund. The set was simple - all the action took place in a living room with French windows opening onto a patio and garden beyond. This posed no problems for the scenic designers, because whatever play they did, the set tended to look like a living room, with French windows opening onto a

patio with a garden beyond.

Dress was modern, which saved a costume problem - and the description of the principal characters matched almost down to a wrinkle the local thespians who were capable of remembering more than two lines together.

He was a clever man, Reverend Arnold Mycock.

I didn't even have to ask who would be playing the lead - Inspector Gerard Danby, tall, gaunt, middle-aged, possessed of a mind brimming with effervescence and wit!

The play was being produced, as always, by Miss Irene Pendlebury, who would also be doubling as Colonel Fraser Marchbanks' housekeeper - a role of considerable importance, as the unfortunate Colonel Marchbanks made a premature exit from life's stage, leaving his housekeeper centre stage, as it were.

"I've prepared a brief outline of the play, without giving anything away of course, hmm," said Mr Mycock, handing me a beautifully-typed sheet of paper.

"Thought you may like to use it on the theatre notes page, hmm."

"Yes. I'm sure we will," I said, taking it from him.

"We'll send a photographer down to dress rehearsal..."

Another sheet of beautifully-typed paper appeared in front of my eyes.

"That is a brief resumé of my writing achievements to date, hmm," intoned the reverend gentleman.

"Thought it may make a piece for your 'People in View' page."

"Er, yes. Fine." I said, taking the proffered notes.

"As I was saying, we'll send a photographer along to the dress rehearsal, then I'll come to the first..."

Once again, a sheet of paper was thrust in front of me.

"Biographical details," said the Reverend Mycock. "Bit about myself. My family. My years in the parish, hmm. Useful to have as background, I thought, hmm."

I took the paper.

"Thank you." I got to my feet.

"Well I don't think I need anything else just now. If I do, I'll give your publicity officer a ring."

I suddenly realised that I'd no idea who the publicity officer was. And I needed to know if only to ensure that the pre-publicity didn't look totally like a hand-out from the Reverend Arnold Mycock Appreciation Society.

"Please do," beamed the Reverend Mycock. "Any time."

"Perhaps you could tell me..." I ventured.

But he interrupted me before I could finish.

"I'm never far away. And if I'm not in, my wife will take a message so I can get back to you, hmm."

*   *   *   *

The Victoria Hall was a warren of rooms and corridors. As well as housing the theatre, which seated some 150, there was a small kitchen; a smaller hall, which during the week accommodated various group meetings; and a room which hosted a youth club on three evenings a week and a pre-school play-group every morning. Upstairs was the games room, which housed a full-size snooker table, two dart boards and a make-shift bar, which was manned, as and when the occasion demanded, by Ted Greensmith from the Ploughman's Tavern.

I left the dress rehearsal picture in the capable hands of Phil, who at the last minute delegated it to his son, Martin, having decided there would be more money in covering a stag night at the Orinoco Club. I thought the less I saw of the Reverend Mycock and Miss Pendlebury before the actual first night, the better.

But the phone on my desk never stopped ringing during the week before "Danby's Darkest Hour" as the Reverend Mycock and Miss Pendlebury and their team of willing helpers bombarded me constantly with snippets of useless information about the play.

No West End production could have had a more persistent publicity machine.

Surely every living being in Lower Greybridge would see the play during its three-night run. Nothing else in the world mattered.

But I was wrong - at least as far as the first night was concerned. For while "Danby's Darkest Hour" was enjoying its world premier to a sell-out audience downstairs, upstairs in the games room it was snooker night for the men.

And come hell and "Danby's Darkest Hour", nothing interfered with that!

*   *   *   *

The theatre was already filling rapidly as I parked my car. I was greeted like a long-lost brother on the door by Mrs Grace Bradshaw, who thrust a raffle ticket into my hand.

"Don't lose that," she trilled. "That's your tea ticket. First interval."

"It includes two arrowroot biscuits or a chocolate digestive."

I was shunted along the line, at the end of which Mrs Jennifer Eckersley handed me a duplicated sheet.

"Programme", she beamed.

"Thank you," I replied, taking it in my other hand.

"That will be one shilling," she said, as she turned to the next in line.

Juggling with my car keys, raffle ticket, programme, I tried to find the right coin in my pocket. Before I did, I dropped my raffle ticket.

"Excuse me," I said as I dived to the ground to retrieve it, narrowly avoiding having a stiletto heel thrust through the back of my hand.

Just then, Mrs Brewer chose to come out of the kitchen, catching me squarely in the hind quarters with the door. I fell forward onto my hands.

"Good heavens," muttered the startled Mrs Brewer.

"Whatever are you doing down there?"

I started to explain, then thought better of it.

"Getting up," I grinned sheepishly.

She shook her head and left me to cope with my embarrassment alone.

I struggled to my feet, pocketed my car keys and raffle ticket, found the elusive coin and approached Mrs Eckersley.

"Yes, dear," she said, looking straight over my left shoulder.

"One shilling," I replied, holding out the coin.

She glanced quickly down at my hand.

"That's right, dear," she said, as if congratulating one of her play-group children on his grasp of the British monetary system.

"For the programme."

"But you've got one, dear," she said. "I gave you one before you started grovelling on the floor."

"I didn't pay for it."

"That's all right," beamed Mrs Eckersley. "You're from the press. You don't have to pay."

"Programmes. One shilling," she trilled again.

I slipped the coin in the direction of my trousers pocket. I heard it clatter to the floor as it missed its intended destination.

I decided to let it rest in peace as I made my way into the rapidly-filling auditorium.

*　　*　　*　　*

The play opened over tea on a Sunday afternoon.

Colonel Fraser Marchbanks was entertaining his two cousins and their respective spouses, each of whom, we quickly gathered, stood to inherit considerable wealth should the old boy meet his demise.

Fussing around as only she could, seeing to their every need, was the redoubtable Miss Irene Pendlebury, for once having discarded her woolly hat in favour of a headscarf.

The plot was obvious, the characters stereotyped almost to the point of caricature, but the audience loved it.

There were two distractions.

The first was whenever a new character made an entrance. The hall erupted into wild applause.

The second came under the heading of noises off - or rather noises above, as the rivalry in the snooker match upstairs became increasingly fierce and raucous.

The dialogue in the play was all but drowned out between the generous applause of the theatre audience and the enthusiastic clapping, stamping and cue banging from the floor above.

But nobody seemed to mind. Lower Greybridge was enjoying itself immensely.

Colonel Fraser Marchbanks lasted longer than I thought he would.

To the very end of the first act, in fact. His end came, not surprisingly,

with his drinking a glass of poisoned wine and going into a prolonged dying swan routine, centre stage.

As the last twitch escaped from his writhing body and he lay prostrate on the floor, the curtain was slowly lowered in what turned out to be the high spot of the play's dramatic content up to that point.

At least, it was slowly lowered to some three feet from the stage, when it appeared to stick momentarily.

"Pull the other one," hissed a disembodied voice, stage left.

The curtain shuddered, then clattered the remaining three feet or so to the stage.

The "dead" Colonel shot up as if he had been stung.

"What the hell are you playing at?" he yelled.

"You could have killed me!"

The sight of a cup of tea and a chocolate digestive biscuit was a delight to behold after that.

*   *   *   *

The rest of the play was taken up with the calling in of Inspector Danby, who got a standing ovation just for making his entrance - and his unravelling of the mystery of who killed the unfortunate Colonel Fraser Marchbanks.

In his efforts to hide the fact that he knew the outcome all along, because he had written the play, the Reverend Mycock did a passable impression of one of the Woodentops.

But W.C.'s words kept stabbing through my brain the minute an unkind thought entered it.

"They're not the Royal friggin' Shakespeare Company. They're doing their best under very trying circumstances to keep alive a theatrical tradition."

I mentally started to compose my review of the play.

Colonel Fraser Marchbanks was played by Terence Fenton; Inspector Danby by Reverend Arnold Mycock... when suddenly, a new character entered the fray.

Inspector Danby was about half-way through eliminating the key suspects, when there was a tap on the French windows.

Miss Pendlebury gave a little smile of recognition.

"Come in, Tommy. It's not locked."

A wizened little man, no more than five feet tall, with three days growth of stubble, bounced into the set.

No one said a word, but all eyes were on him.

"He did it," he cried gleefully.

I was just wondering how this character, who hadn't put in an appearance of any sort in the entire action, could have known who the murderer was, when the audience erupted.

"Dave did it!" squealed grizzly beard in delight.

It was becoming curiouser and curiouser. I looked down at the programme. There was no Dave on the cast list.

The characters on stage joined in the spontaneous round of applause.

And without another word, he went out the same way he came in, carefully closing the French windows behind him.

The Reverend Mycock turned his attention back to Fraser Marchbanks' first cousin.

"And you laddie...you wouldn't have the backbone to drown a blind kitten, let alone murder your cousin."

I turned to Mrs Tuffnell sitting next to me.

"Who was that?" I asked.

"Tommy Shipton," she hissed.

"He's not in the programme."

"Course he isn't." she snapped, intent on following the action on stage.

I waited a respectable couple of minutes before raising the subject again.

"What was he doing there?" I asked.

Mrs Tuffnell glared at me.

"He came to give the snooker result," she snapped back impatiently.

"What do you think he was doing? Honestly, call yourself a reporter!"

* * * *

I watched the rest of the production in silence, as it ground to its predictable end.

"What did you think of it?" I asked Mrs Tuffnelll after the cast had taken twelve curtain calls.

"Ending was all wrong," she said, tightlipped.

"It seemed all right to me," I offered. "A bit contrived, perhaps. But believable."

"Believable?" she flared. "Believable?"

"Never in a million years. You know who did it, don't you?"

"Simon Marchbanks," I replied. I had paid that much attention.

"That was Harry Clewthorpe from the Post Office," scoffed Mrs Tuffnell in disgust.

"And you can take it from me. If there's a proper gentleman in this village, it's him. He wouldn't harm a fly, he wouldn't. Let alone kill his own cousin."

"Not in a million years!"

* * * *

The following Thursday morning, I reacted like a coiled spring every time the phone on my desk rang, waiting for the call from W.C. that would inevitably follow the call from the Reverend Mycock as sure as night follows day.

The man's greatest literary achievement, and I couldn't find it in me to say anything praiseworthy about it.

Bearing in mind Walter's cautionary words, my review of "Danby's Darkest Hour" amounted to little more than a run-down of the printed programme.

The call came at quarter-to-eleven.

I tapped on W.C.'s door frame and waited for the gruff invitation to enter.

"Come in. Come in," the editor beamed.

"Just had Mycock on the phone."

I shifted uneasily from one leg to the other. He was actually enjoying this.

"Delighted with your piece."

"Really?" I said in astonishment.

"But it didn't say anything."

"Ahh, but it did," said Walter with a broad smile. "For one thing you managed to get his name into it four times."

"But the pay-off...well he couldn't have been more delighted if you'd have given him an Oscar. Even if it was a little white lie."

"A little white lie?" I protested.

"If there was one line in the whole piece that was written straight from the heart, that was it."

It really was an evening I will never forget!

9

WALKING through Greybridge town centre with Walter Piggin was something akin to being in attendance at a Royal visit. He was known by just about every member of the adult population, and it could quite easily take twenty minutes to cover a hundred yards on market days.

A nod here. A wave there. A pause to renew a faded acquaintanceship with a firm handshake and a vague promise to be in touch again soon. A few warm, heart-felt words with an old and trusted friend of long standing, of which Walter had many.

He was the finest ambassador the *Pioneer* - or any other organisation come to that - could have had. Well respected, well trusted and well known, he had regarded himself as chief standard bearer of the company ensign since the day he joined the paper.

"We are more than just a newspaper," he would say with pride, stretching his waistcoat nearly to bursting point as he puffed out his chest.

"We are an institution."

Fine words from a dedicated man.

He was right, of course. The more I came to know the people of Greybridge and the more they came to know me, I found that stories grew out of the easy relationships that prevailed. I became accessible.

Quite often I was asked to do little things that were nothing to do with the newspaper. I would frequently be asked to fill in the odd form for an elderly person. Or to call in at the Post Office or supermarket for someone.

And I think it was true to say that with the possible exception of Gary, that we all saw we had a role to play in the community. It was expected of us. Exactly as spelled out by Walter Charlesworth Piggin.

The annoying thing was that he didn't seem to be aware of anyone's efforts but his own.

Mrs Grace Dalrymple Hogg, wife of our revered proprietor, was a sharp-featured, slightly-built lady in her mid-thirties.

She was well-groomed from the top of her carefully coiffured auburn-tinted hair to the tip of her hand-made shoes.

As a result of her social standing in the community, she was involved with just about every committee and organisation in Greybridge, and our paths frequently crossed as I came across her in one capacity or another.

The big tragedy was that Mrs Grace Dalrymple Hogg had no individual character of her own. Although she adequately filled the bill in whatever role she was playing, she had all the personal charm and charisma of a fishmonger's slab.

And she saw her own family in the same way.

Her husband was the provider, a pillar of support to her.

Their ten-year-old twin daughters, Kim and Naomi were simply two more possessions to boast about. Their sports prowess. Their academic achievements.

I quickly came to the conclusion that there could be nothing in the world that she cared for for itself.

But I was wrong.

*　　*　　*　　*

When Grace Dalrymple Hogg took it upon herself to visit the office, it was usually because she wanted something in her capacity as chairman of this, patron of that, publicity officer of the other.

Walter was in the reporters' room, when the phone rang.

Dawn answered it.

"Is Mr Piggin with you?" came the cheery voice of Christine from the front office.

Dawn turned to the editor.

"Mrs Dalrymple Hogg for you," she said.

W.C. grunted and moved to take the phone.

"Not on the phone. She's here. On her way up."

Walter moved as if he had a wasp down his trousers. He quickly straightened his tie, scratched feverishly at a spot in a vain attempt to remove it, brushed an imaginary speck of dust off his jacket and made for his own office.

That normally would be the last we saw of him for an hour or so, as he paid his due respects to the proprietor's lady, instructed Christine to get out the best cups and saucers - both of them - ordered the lemon tea to be sent up, and listened attentively to Grace's request for space in the *Pioneer* to publicise her latest pet cause.

But this time, it was different.

Within five minutes, Walter was back, this time closely followed by Grace herself, who didn't so much walk into the office as make an entrance on a cloud of Chanel No 5.

"If I could just have your attention for a moment," said the editor with as much dignity and authority as he could muster.

"Now you're all aware of the efforts I make to try to impress on you our need to keep a high profile in society."

He received no answer.

"Well I'm happy to say that once again we have an opportunity to provide a service above and beyond the publication of our newspaper."

Still no response. We were waiting for him to get to the point.

"I think I'd better ask them, Walter," interjected Grace.

"I haven't got all day."

"As you wish," muttered W.C. He dutifully took one step backwards, knocking the telephone off Dawn's desk.

"The fact is," went on Mrs Dalrymple Hogg, "my husband and I are taking the family off on holiday for a few days, and we seem to have overlooked one tiny little detail." She paused for effect.

"Max".

"I wouldn't worry about that," said Dawn brightly. "It probably won't rain anyway."

Mrs Dalrymple Hogg shot her a glance that would have penetrated armoured steel.

"I am referring to my West Highland terrier."

"Aubrey completely forgot to contact the kennels, and now, at such short notice, well there's no way they can accommodate him. Not even for me."

She beamed at the assembled throng.

"So, as I so often do, I turned to the most resourceful man in Greybridge."

She turned her gaze on Walter Piggin, who was waiting for her to reveal this colossus of society.

"My dear friend, Walter. I thought if anyone can find a way out of my predicament, he can."

Walter preened.

"You're looking for someone to have your dog while you're on holiday?" I asked.

Mrs Dalrymple Hogg nodded.

"I am indeed".

"Mrs Piggin would have him, of course…"

"Without question," agreed Walter.

"But unfortunately her allergy precludes her."

Gary looked at Walter as if he had just materialised from the mists of time.

"Allergy?"

Walter shifted uncomfortably.

"Er, yes. She has this allergy to fur. Animal fur."

"Dogs don't have fur," offered Dawn brightly. "They have hair."

W.C. shot her a withering glance.

"That as well," he said quickly. "Anything to do with animals. She comes out in a rash. Lumps all over her legs and arms. Her eyes start running..."

"All right, Walter. I think we have the picture", interrupted Grace.

"The fact is that Walter thought that if the worst came to the worst and we couldn't find anyone, well one of his staff may know someone."

She paused to gauge the reaction of what she had just said.

There was a silence. Surprisingly, Gary was the first to break it.

"One of us, you mean?"

Mrs Dalrymple Hogg beamed.

"Well of course, if you're offering. Mind you, it must be someone who loves dogs. And adores West Highland terriers."

Gary grinned at her.

"No problem."

I couldn't believe my ears.

"I adore dogs. And my Fang loves West Highland terriers."

Mrs Dalrymple Hogg looked distinctly uncomfortable.

"Fang?" she asked.

"My alsatian," replied Gary, inspecting his finger nails.

"He eats nothing else."

Mrs Dalrymple Hogg started to turn the colour of her auburn-tinted hair.

She rounded on W.C.

"I came here hoping for assistance in my time of need. It seems I chose the wrong place."

"No," spluttered Walter. "Definitely not. I can assure you my dear lady that if all else fails, my staff will look after your dear little dog. Even if they have to take it in turns."

Mrs Dalrymple Hogg pointed a shaky finger in the direction of Gary.

"I wouldn't let my dear little Max within a mile of him," she thundered.

"If he was the last person on earth."

"Er, no. Well he wouldn't be included of course," said Walter quickly.

"Now come along. The tea will be getting cold."

With a last, cool look in the direction of Gary, Mrs Dalrymple Hogg turned on her heel and left the room, with Walter in hot pursuit.

Dawn looked at Gary in some surprise.

"How long have you had an alsatian?"

Gary switched his attention to the evening paper.

"I'm looking after it for a friend," he replied off-handedly.

"How long for?" I asked incredulously. I wouldn't have trusted Gary to look after a hibernating tortoise.

Gary flicked the paper open at the diary page.

"For as long as that dreadful woman persists in looking for a home for that animated mop head of hers."

The following morning, the editor came into the reporters' room with a grin as wide as the Colliers Wharf.

"You'll be very happy to hear," he beamed, "that the wife of our proprietor has found a temporary home for her dog. Her next door-but-two neighbours are taking their caravan to a farm for a few days, and they've agreed to take Max with them and keep him until the Dalrymple Hoggs get back. So she won't be calling on you to help her out of her predicament after all."

"But she does wish me to convey her thanks to you, nevertheless. Your public spiritedness in so readily offering your services didn't go unnoticed."

He turned his gaze full on Gary.

"Especially yours."

*　*　*　*

It was about eleven o'clock before I arrived at the office on Monday morning. I had calls to make. People to see.

The office was empty. Elliot Forbes was coaxing Inspector Crabtree to a third cup of cocoa over at the police station, in an attempt to stretch the end of his police calls to coincide with opening time.

Gary, as usual, hadn't put in an appearance. While Dawn had been in and gone out again to a Flower Club coffee morning.

Even Walter Piggin was out. He'd gone off to meet the Borough Surveyor to find out if there was any truth in a rumour that a housing association had bought up the last of the town's allotments.

I made myself a coffee and sat down to write up the diary for the week. I had been working for about twenty minutes, when I heard the downstairs door clatter open, followed by Christine's surprised voice.

"What in the name of mercy have you got there?" Her dulcet tones carried up two flights of stairs with the ease of a hot knife going through butter.

I didn't quite catch Walter's muffled reply. But I did know it was the editor.

And he was far from happy.

Suddenly, there was a patter on the stairs, and a yell from our esteemed editor.

"Come back here, you brute. Come here…"

The patter on the stairs was drowned as Walter's size tens did their best to carry his ageing frame up towards his office, two at a time.

"Come here, you fiend," he yelled, before the general commotion headed for his office.

I got up and went to see what was going on.

As I went through the door, a white ball of animated hair leapt at me, and Walter's coat stand, to which the animal was tethered, crashed across his desk.

"You idiot," he yelled at me. "I nearly had him settled."

I looked down. Standing on its hind legs, pawing at my trouser leg, its tail wagging so quickly you could hardly see it, was a distinctly off-white West Highland terrier.

"Where did you get this from?" I asked with a smile.

"You might well ask," muttered Walter, as he tried to haul his coat stand upright again.

"That, believe it or not, is the dreaded Max."

"What are *you* doing with him?" I asked in surprise.

"I thought they'd made other arrangements."

"They had," groaned Walter, desperation in his voice. "He must have run away."

"Run away?"

"I was driving along Parkside Crescent, wasn't I. Past the Dalrymple Hogg's house. And there he was. Having the time of his life with six or seven other dogs. No collar. Nothing."

"But how do you know it's Max?"

"I'd know Max anywhere, wouldn't I. I've seen him often enough."

"And when I called him, he came to me like a shot."

The little dog was beginning to settle down as I rubbed its sharp little ears.

"But I thought the Dalrymple Hogg's neighbours were taking him away with them. In their caravan."

"They were. But I don't think they were going far."

"He must have slipped his collar and found his way home again."

I looked down at the friendly little dog.

"Well if you want me to keep an eye on the office while you take it back to them..."

"I don't know where they've gone," screeched Walter.

"Nor does anyone else."

"So what are you going to do with it?" I asked.

Just then, we heard the downstairs door open and close, followed by Dawn's voice in the front office.

I glanced towards W.C. as Dawn came up the stairs. He glanced towards me. The look of relief on his face was plain to see.

"Er...Dawn," he called.

Dawn appeared in the doorway.

Walter turned on his most benevolent smile.

"I have a little job for you, my dear."

*   *   *   *

Max seemed to settle down very quickly with Dawn and her mother.

The little dog was bathed. Dawn bought him a new collar and lead, and they both grew quite attached to him.

"It's going to be quite a wrench to give him back," she told the editor on the day the Dalrymple Hoggs were due home.

"I can't tell you how grateful I am," said Walter.

"If Mrs Dalrymple Hogg had come home to find her little Max had disappeared, it would have been me who would have been in for a dog's life from now on."

"You?" Dawn looked at him quizzically.

"She wouldn't have given Aubrey a moment's peace."

"And who would Aubrey take it out on?"

Dawn nodded. She well understood how the chain of command worked. And she didn't need telling who the editor would take it out on, either.

Fortunately, it hadn't come to that.

"I'll take him back about mid-day," she said brightly.

"Er, no. That won't be necessary," said Walter hurriedly as Dawn prepared to leave the office.

"I thought that, well, as I was the one who found him and certain explanations are necessary... And I don't want to cause any bad feeling between Grace and her friends, I mean after all, they were only trying to do her a favour..."

"You'll take him back?" interrupted Dawn.

"I think it may be better," agreed Walter.

*   *   *   *

The Mitre was more busy than usual by one o'clock.

Dawn and I were in the habit of popping in to keep Elliot company for half an hour, then we would make our excuses and leave as we passed him on to whoever we could find to take him off our hands until closing time.

It was fast approaching the witching hour.

"My shout," proclaimed Elliot for the third time, though he had yet to pay for a round.

"Set 'em up again Alec."

Alec dutifully filled Elliot's pint pot and my half pint pot, and was about to open Dawn's bottle of grapefruit juice when Elliot, with split-second timing honed to perfection over many years, broke in.

"Nature calls," he bleated. "Back in a sec."

And he was away through the throng in the direction of the gents.

Alec put the grapefruit juice down and held out his hand.

"It's Elliot's round," I protested.

"Elliot isn't here, is he?" muttered Alec.

"He never bloody well is," I thought.

I passed across a five pound note.

"How does he manage to get away with it?" I moaned. "Every time."

Dawn smiled.

"Practise. Cheers."

We were about to head for a vacant table, when W.C. hurried in, his face the colour of a Mediterranean sunset.

His sharp little eyes flicked over the unfamiliar faces until they alighted on me and Dawn.

He bore through the crowd like a mole on heat, appearing between us as if by magic.

"Thank goodness I've caught you," he gulped.

"I want one of you to phone the police station."

Dawn looked shocked. She'd never seen the editor in such a state.

"Whatever's happened?" she asked in some alarm.

Walter's moustache bristled.

"That blasted dog."

"You've not lost him again?" I said incredulously.

"No, I haven't," he bellowed, his complexion turning a shade darker.

"I wish I'd never set eyes on the wretched animal in the first place."

"But what's happened?" urged Dawn again, her concern heightened now she knew it wasn't Walter who was in jeopardy, but the dog.

"Where's Max?"

"I took the dog back to the Dalrymple Hoggs," W.C. stammered.

We waited for him to go on.

"I rang the door bell. Grace answered it."

"And so did the children."

"And so did Max!"

Dawn and I looked at each other.

"Max? But *you* had Max."

I tried to stifle the laugh welling up inside me as the truth dawned.

"You mean the dog you picked up and brought back to the office..."

Walter choked back his embarrassment and turned to Dawn.

"Get on the phone to the police," he pleaded.

"See if anyone has reported losing a West Highland terrier in the last few days."

"Vicinity of Parkside Crescent."

*   *   *   *

Walter Charlesworth Piggin was wiping the earpiece of his telephone with a paper tissue as I went into his office.

His paper clips, stapler, hole punch, pens and pencils were all lined up like a motley troop of soldiers awaiting inspection on his desk in front of him.

He had the contented smile of a man at peace with the world.

Getting the dog back to its tearful young owner had been no problem.

A quiet word in the ear of Sergeant Blacker, and within an hour the dog was home, no questions asked.

The family had been so delighted to have it back.

"You didn't get a photograph then?" I asked.

"Photograph?" The editor carefully replaced the telephone handset.

"Of the little girl being reunited with her lost pet. It would have made a great picture."

Walter glared at me.

"Only trying to be constructive," I said.

"If Dawn had taken the dog back. Told the family that it had been handed over to her at the *Pioneer* office which isn't entirely a lie – well, if it hadn't been for the *Pioneer,* that little girl may never have seen her dog again."

"Now that really is involvement in the community!"

But Walter had lost interest.

That spot on his tie really was proving troublesome!

10

WHEN Walter Piggin sauntered into the office on a Thursday afternoon, tugging at his left ear-lobe, passing complimentary remarks about that week's paper and generally appearing to be in a most affable mood, it spelled trouble for someone.

The first time I came across this phenomenon, it was me!

I didn't recognise the signs, and no one thought to enlighten me.

Gary was hurling darts at a picture from that week's paper of the lady chairperson of the local Conservative Association, with whom he had had a slight altercation earlier in the day over his reporting – or rather mis-reporting – of a constituency meeting.

Dawn was carefully folding the notes from her pay packet and tucking them into their respective pockets in her purse.

She was very astute when it came to money, was Dawn.

I was glancing through the *Herald Weekly* to see what we had missed, if anything, of the past week's activities in Greybridge.

Elliot had not yet returned from lunch, even though it was nearly four o'clock.

"I was driving past the floral display outside the Town Hall this morning," volunteered W.C. to no one in particular.

"It really is marvellous what can be done with the right plants, these days."

I nodded agreement.

"And it's no longer confined to the Parks Department. Oh, no."

"Because people have found that gardening can be fun."

"I mean would the garden centres have been so successful if gardening hadn't been so popular?"

I shook my head at what seemed to be an appropriate point in the editor's monologue.

He tugged more ferociously on his ear lobe, giving his face a slightly distorted and more sinister look than usual.

"I don't know if any of you have visited the garden centre on the Woodstone Road…"

I looked up from the *Herald Weekly*. W.C. was at last straying into familiar waters.

"I go there quite a lot," I offered.

"Really?" the editor beamed.

It was if I had suddenly disclosed the secret of eternal life.

"I didn't realise you were a gardener."

"I'm not," I replied, "I go to the coffee shop there"

I turned back to the *Herald Weekly.*

"I'm very pleased to hear it,"said Walter releasing his long-suffering ear-lobe at last.

"You're just the person."

"For what?" I queried.

"Miss Grasscroft has an advertising feature planned for next week. She wants some editorial to go with it. You know the kind of thing. Say what you like about the place, so long as its complimentary."

I started to protest.

"I'm sure one of the others…"

But Walter cut me short.

"If you can let Miss Grasscroft have your copy by tomorrow afternoon."

And he turned and left the room.

I turned to complain to Dawn. She wasn't there.

There was no one there but me.

As soon as the editor had made it clear that he wanted one volunteer to step forward, the others had neatly taken one step back.

*　　*　　*　　*

Hilda Grasscroft was, to be kind, a well-built woman in her early fifties. About 16 stones well-built. She wore her greying hair in a tight little bun at the back of her head, and the long, full dresses she always wore gave her the appearance of a walking tent. She had been in charge of advertising for over 20 years, and was pure gold to the accountants in whose hands the fortunes of the *Pioneer* ebbed and flowed.

And one of the favourite weapons in her armoury was the advertising feature.

When I got back to the office on Friday morning, after my visit to the garden centre, I was waylaid by Miss Grasscroft before I had reached the stairs.

She proceeded to tell me the names of all the advertisers she had managed to rope in in support of the garden centre, and to remind me to mention each one of them by name somewhere in the piece I was about to write.

To underline her concern, she was to phone me every half hour to remind me, as I tried desperately to make an interesting feature out of a collection of pot plants and garden ornaments, while Gary and Dawn were enjoying what was traditionally the slacker end of the week in comparative peace and quiet.

But I was a quick learner, and Thursday afternoons became a game of cat and mouse to avoid such chores in future whenever Walter Piggin made his ear-tugging presence felt.

But try as I may, I was no match for Gary, who had the distinct talent of being able to vanish from the scene seconds before Walter got to the point, and who had so far spurned every effort to get him to recognise that Hilda Grasscroft even existed.

I eventually had to come to terms with the fact that whenever there was an advertising feature to do, it was all down to me or Dawn.

I was convinced that the day Gary got lumbered with such a task would be the day the earth opened up and swallowed us all!

*   *   *   *

Driving past the Town Hall to the office some weeks later, I glanced across at the floral display. It was an involuntary action programmed into my brain every time I drove past it, since it was used in such a devious way to get me to write the garden centre advertising feature.

But on this morning, there was something different about it. My view wasn't obscured as it usually was by the two bollards in the middle of the read which marked the centre point of the pedestrian crossing. They had both apparently been unceremoniously removed in some haste, judging by the shower of broken glass surrounding the island where they had once stood.

I never gave it another thought – until midway through the morning, when there was a phone call for Gary, who was even more late than usual.

"Can I take a message?" I offered. "He should be in any time".

He should have been in any time for the past two hours.

"Tell him Fran called. Greasby's Garage."

"He's looking at something over four hundred quid."

"New wing, headlamp, work on the door panel. And he's probably done the radiator in."

"He must have given it a fair smack," I replied.

"Oh, he did. Lucky devil."

"Lucky?"

"Dead lucky. Lucky there was no one else involved."

"And lucky there was no one around to see what happened."

"Anyway, tell him what the damage is and I'll hold fire till I hear from him. See you."

I replaced the phone and was still thinking about what Fran had said when Gary walked in.

He crossed to his desk without a word.

"Gary," I called across.

"If you're going to state the obvious and tell me I'm late, you can forget it," he snapped.

"I've nearly walked my legs off this morning."

"No car?" I tried to sound casually surprised.

Gary shrugged.

"Wouldn't start this morning."

"Had to get it towed in."

"Engine trouble?" I said in some surprise.

"That's right," brazened Gary. "You know how it is."

"I know exactly how it is," I volunteered.

"I've just had Fran on the phone."

Gary went a couple of shades paler.

"Fran!"

"He asked me to tell you that you'd be looking at upwards of four hundred pounds for the repairs."

"It needs a new wing, headlamp, door panel..."

Gary cut me short.

"*How* much?"

He had gone another shade paler.

"Four hundred pounds," I repeated.

"It can't be worth much more than that."

Gary whistled through his clenched teeth.

"I don't suppose there's any connection between your little accident and the demolition of the bollards outside the Town Hall this morning," I probed.

Gary looked up sharply.

"I don't know what you mean," he said, turning away.

That was the end of the conversation, I thought.

I was wrong. Gary turned back.

"It was only one. An articulated lorry carted the other one yesterday afternoon."

*   *   *   *

It took Gary some twenty minutes to summon up the courage to phone Fran back, explain that he was temporarily financially embarrassed and to ask him to hold on to the car to await further instructions. By mid-afternoon, he was as chirpy as a cricket again.

He had managed to avoid going out on at least three jobs, arguing lack of suitable transport.

By tea time, it seemed that Gary would not find being without a car for a while too big a problem. In fact, it was beginning to look as if he might actually enjoy it.

But on Wednesday morning, that changed dramatically.

He got a call from his latest girl-friend, Sarah, to discuss arrangements for the weekend.

The seriousness of Gary's predicament hit him between the eyes like a thunderbolt.

He picked up the phone and dialled Greasby's Garage.

"Fran? Gary. I don't suppose you've done anything with the car yet?"

"Yes, I know what I said… No. I haven't been able to raise the four hundred. Not yet. But I'm working on it…"

"I see. You're not. Well thanks a lot, pal. I'll be in touch."

For the rest of the afternoon, we heard hardly a word from Gary, as his brain turned over the various options he had before him for getting transport in time for weekend.

By the expression on his face at five-thirty, and his reaction to my reminder that he had a council meeting to attend at eight, it was proving an insurmountable problem, even for him.

*   *   *   *

On Thursday morning, to my surprise, he was at work when I arrived at the office.

'At work' for Gary meant he was half-way through the morning papers. I was about to ask him if he had solved his transport problem, when the phone rang. Gary leapt to answer it.

"Hi, Christine." He listened intently.

"She's in, is she? Right. Thanks."

"Put me through, will you?"

Dawn and I waited, ears straining.

"Miss Grasscroft? Hello, Hilda. It's Gary. Editorial…"

"I've got something I want to discuss with you."

"I wondered if you might be free for a drink at lunchtime?"

Dawn and I looked at each other in disbelief.

"I'll give you a shout about half twelve. See you."

Gary replaced the phone and immersed himself once again in his papers, the trace of a smile tugging at the corners of his mouth. We waited eagerly for an explanation.

We were to be disappointed.

*   *   *   *

It was turned half past two before Gary put in an appearance after lunch.

And he had a grin as wide as Greybridge Downs.

Half an hour later, Walter made his entrance, tugging at the ear lobe, droning on about the marvellous work that was being done to give old housing a new lease of life.

I knew what was coming. Two enterprising lads had started up a company renovating old houses in the town, and Hilda Grasscroft had been beavering away to get some advertising from them for weeks. I tried to be evasive, but to my surprise, Gary took up the running. Walter was delighted.

"It's very gratifying to know that you are so well informed," he said with a smile.

"And I never realised you had such a keen interest in the restoration of old property."

Gary returned the smile.

"And I can't think of anyone better suited to do this week's advertising feature," beamed the editor, as he delivered his coup de grace.

I couldn't help wondering if Gary had suffered some kind of bump on the head during his early morning argument with the traffic bollards. It was the only explanation I could think of for his current attitude.

"There's nothing I'd like better," said Gary, the smile still firmly fixed on his face.

Walter turned to leave the office.

"Unfortunately..."

Walter stopped in his tracks.

"Unfortunately what?" he growled.

"Unfortunately I've something else on tomorrow," replied Gary casually.

The editor's colour started to darken visibly as he tried to control himself.

"Advertising" he bellowed "is the lifeblood of this newspaper, young man. And don't you ever forget it."

Gary was completely unruffled.

"I couldn't agree with you more," he said.

"That's why I regarded it as my duty to put up a certain idea to Hilda...
Miss Grasscroft. Even if it does mean I shall now be writing one of these
advertising features every week."

Walter couldn't believe his ears. Neither, for that matter, could I. Gary
paused for the full effect of his revelation.

"Starting this week, I shall be doing a weekly road test on a quality
used car from one of our local dealers."

"In return, they will double their advertising space that week."

"Hilda... Miss Grasscroft, has sounded out one or two garages on the
idea and they're falling over themselves to get in on the act."

W.C.'s face lit up with pleasure.

"I don't know what to say. You were the last person in the world I
would have marked down as having the interests of this paper at heart. But,
well, what can I say?"

He turned to me.

"I'm sure you can handle the building restoration feature."

He moved to the doorway.

"If there's anything you need to know, I'm sure Gary will help you out."

I looked at Gary with deep suspicion. The editor may have been taken
in, but I certainly wasn't.

"And what's in this for you, then?"

Gary looked hurt.

"I try to do something for the paper, and what thanks do I get?"

"So you're doing your first road test tomorrow?"

"Volvo estate. From Greybridge Motors. Two years old. Picking her up
at lunchtime. Now if you'll excuse me, I do have a phone call to make."

He dialled Sarah's number.

Dawn, who had been silent until then, but had viewed Gary's motives
with as much suspicion as I had, interrupted him.

"When do you have to have this car back, then?"

"Same as all the others," grinned Gary.

"Monday morning."

* * * *

By ten o'clock on Monday morning, Gary had his piece written about
the Volvo ready to go in the paper. And he set about his day to day work
with a new verve.

He had obviously had an enjoyable weekend with Sarah. And his
transport hadn't cost him a penny. He even had a tankful of petrol thrown in.

He was delighted with his little scheme.

And because the local garages could see the potential of the idea, Gary was going to be able to pick and choose his own vehicle every weekend from now on. Riding high on the euphoria of his success, he phoned Fran.

"Fran? Gary. About my motor... No, I haven't managed to raise the four hundred. I've got a suggestion to make."

"I know it's taking up valuable garage space. Will you just listen for a minute. Why don't you put the thing right at your expense..."

He held the phone away from his ear to avoid the torrent of abuse that came from it.

"If you'll just listen," said Gary at last. "You put the car right, sell it, keep your four hundred and give me what you've got left..."

"Yes, of course I'm serious. I can't see myself needing it again."

"Not for the foreseeable future, certainly. You will?"

"Well don't sound so bloody pleased about it. I'll see you."

He replaced the phone, then picked it up again.

Two more calls, then he could get down to work.

First Sarah. Then Riverside Motors.

Perhaps they'd have something a bit special this weekend.

*   *   *   *

Gary's optimism about his scheme proved to be well-founded.

Each weekend he would collect the car of his choice from a different garage, then return it on his way into the office on Monday morning.

Each Thursday, his glowing report about the car would appear in the paper, and within a couple of hours, it would be sold.

It was some four weeks after Gary's scheme had got off the ground that Sarah mentioned the point-to point meeting.

It was to be held at One Oak Farm on the other side of Grey Tor on the Sunday, and Sarah and Gary had been invited to join a party of a dozen or so of Sarah's county set friends for a barbecue at the end of the afternoon's racing.

Gary had jumped at the opportunity.

"Well it'll certainly be different," I said, when he told me about the weekend.

"Different? I've been to hundreds of barbecues."

"I meant driving a Land Rover. If you're going to a point-to-point, you don't want your average run of the mill old banger. Not for something like that. You've got to look the part."

I deliberately omitted to say which part!

Gary smiled. He picked up the phone and dialled a number.

"Barrowclough's?" inquired Gary brightly. "Good morning. This is the *Pioneer.*"

"I wonder if I could speak to Mr Barrowclough."

"Oh, I see. Well perhaps I could tell you what it's about..."

"You've probably read our 'Best Deals on Wheels' feature..."

"Yes, there was a car I had in mind. Three years old, maroon. You've had it in about a month now. I just thought it may be sticking."

"Just the thing to benefit from a piece in our column."

Gary smiled.

"That's right. That's the one. The convertible."

* * * *

Gary collected the car as usual on Friday afternoon. It was nearer four years old than three, it had done a high mileage, and was showing some signs of its age. But when Gary roared off in it for the weekend there was no doubt he felt ten feet tall.

I saw him a couple of times on Saturday afternoon flashing round the town. The convertible had certainly done something for his image. There was no doubt that Gary firmly believed that this was definitely the life to which he had been born.

Sunday morning was bright and warm, but as the day wore on, the heat became more intense, until towards late afternoon it became rather too clammy for comfort.

I had been out walking and was about ten minutes from home when I heard the first distant rumbling of thunder.

Over the next few minutes, the heavy, grey sky became darker and heavier. I quickened my step and made it to within a couple of hundred yards of home before the huge drops of rain started to hit the pavement with a resounding splat, at first only spasmodic, but as I put the key in the front door, the sky was lit up by a blinding flash of lightning and the still air was rent almost immediately with a deafening crack of thunder which turned out to be the signal for the heavens to open,

I was grateful I had nothing more ambitious planned for that night than a quiet evening in, with only the television for company.

Early the next morning I was wrenched from a deep, satisfying sleep by what seemed like every fire engine in the universe clanging through my brain. As I slowly came round, I reached out to put the alarm off. Still the bells peeled out their angry message. Gradually, in my dim state of consciousness, I realised it wasn't the alarm clock. It was the telephone. I hauled myself out of bed. The clock showed twenty five past seven. I absently picked up the phone. Any last strains of sub-consciousness were swept away as I heard Gary's agitated voice at the other end.

"What kept you?" he bellowed.

I started to explain about the process of sleep, which most law-abiding respectable citizens habitually practised. But he wasn't interested.

"I need a favour," he urged, then quickly moderated his voice.

"No panic. But can you get over to One Oak Farm?"

"One Oak Farm?" I queried.

"With a strong tow rope."

"Tow rope?" I repeated, my brain trying desperately to click into first gear.

"But..."

I was cut short before I could say any more.

"Just come. Now," pleaded Gary.

"It's a matter of life and death. I'll explain later."

"A matter of life and death? But whose..."

"Mine," he conceded.

*　*　*　*

It took me no more than twenty minutes to drive over to One Oak Farm. It was a glorious morning, the colours of the landscape having been refreshed by the rain of the previous night, and now highlighted by the gentle wash of the early morning sunlight.

As I took the unmade track heading from Grey Tor towards the farm, I began to regret ever answering the phone, as my ancient Morris 1000 bumped and jolted along, groaning at every impact, the muddy water splashing window high as it ploughed through the morass.

The signs of the previous day's point-to-point were still in evidence, as I negotiated the final bend before the road fell away in front of me to the farm below, and I was suddenly confronted with the reason for Gary's desperation.

Standing alone and undignified in the slush of what twenty four hours before had been a crowded car park, was the mud-splattered outline of what had once been a gleaming, maroon status symbol.

Perched on the bonnet, like some grotesque mascot, his shoes and socks nowhere to be seen, trousers rolled up to his knees, was Gary.

He slid to the ground as he saw me approaching. I stopped the car on the road as he paddled towards me.

"What happened?" I asked.

"Don't ask," muttered Gary. "Just get me out of here."

I looked closer at Gary's mud-splattered clothes, his unshaven features, his tired, deep-set eyes.

"You look as if you've been here all night."

"I have," mumbled Gary. "I slept in the car. Well it's bugger all use for anything else."

"I'm not with you."

"We were having a great time, weren't we. Then the heavens opened."

"We packed up. Someone shouted 'Everyone back to my place' and made a dash for it."

"But Sarah?" I interrupted. "What happened to her?"

Gary looked pained.

"The last I saw of her, she was heading for a Land Rover with a couple of mates."

"They all roared off into the night. Except me. I was stuck fast."

I almost felt sorry for him. Almost.

"I told you you'd have been better off with a Land Rover," I offered, not very helpfully.

"Thanks a lot," said Gary. "Well come on…"

He indicated the gateway to the field.

"You can forget that," I countered. "If I drive through there, that'll be two of us stuck."

"You can't leave me here," pleaded Gary. "I've got to get the car back."

"I'll nip down to the farm."

"Get them to bring a tractor out. You'll be out in no time."

"Good thinking," said Gary, showing the first glimmer of hope I had seen in his face that morning.

"Then you can give me a tow into Greybridge."

"Me?" I said in some surprise. "You won't need me once you get out of that lot."

Gary looked defeated again.

"There is another slight problem," he admitted.

"While I was trying to get the brute out, I burned out the clutch!"

*　　*　　*　　*

We didn't see Gary back in the office until well after lunch on the Monday.

By which time, Barrowclough's had been on to Hilda Grasscroft. And Hilda had been on to Walter Piggin. While the rest of us took the slightest excuse to get out of the office.

When Gary did decide to show his face, the dust had settled

sufficiently for the cost of his weekend escapade to be roughly assessed.

One lost major motor dealer advertiser.

One near-nervous breakdown for Hilda Grasscroft.

Ten years off Walter Piggin's life expectancy.

And an estimated bill of nearly three hundred pounds for recovering, replacing clutch and other repairs to put the car back into a saleable condition.

On Thursday morning, the phone rang.

It was for Gary. It seemed that there was still one garage in the whole of the Greybridge valley that had not yet heard of the disastrous experiences of Barrowclough's Quality Used cars at the hands of Gary.

That was Entwhistle Greenhalgh of Lower Greybridge.

Old Mr Greenhalgh must have been eighty if he was a day.

The day to day running of the garage was now in the hands of his two sons. But old Entwhistle still liked to take an active interest.

"I've been reading your car reports in the *Pioneer,*" he yelled in a pitch we could hear the other side of the office, as he assumed everyone was as hard of hearing as he was.

"I was wondering if you were fixed up for this weekend."

"Only we've got a a lovely two-year-old…"

Before he could enlighten Gary any further, he slammed the phone down with such a crack it split the handset!

11

SUMMERLEA Residential Home was a large house of Derbyshire stone set in some four acres of ground which overlooked rolling farmland to the north of Greybridge.

At one time, it had been the home of Sir Gerald Croston, founder of Croston's Tile Works, and his family, when it had echoed to the sounds of bustling activity as those in service attended to the day to day requirements of Sir Gerald and his wife, Emily, their six children and the many business acquaintances who were frequent house guests at Summerlea over the years.

And indeed, in those days it was a dynasty that seemed set to rule at Summerlea for ever.

But death duties had changed all that.

The family was fragmented, and now there wasn't a living descendant of Sir Gerald within twenty miles of Greybridge. For many years, the old house had been left to the ravages of time.

It had a brief, new-found lease of life towards the end of the second world war, when it was requisitioned by His Majesty's Government as temporary quarters for convalescing soldiers.

For some years afterwards it became an isolation hospital, eventually being vacated, presumably to be left to decay until the bulldozers moved in to put it out of its misery and write the final chapter in its chequered history.

But the grand old building was to be spared such an ignominious end when a saviour arrived in the nick of time in the shape of the county social services department.

The structure was still sound, and with the minimum of cosmetic work and refurbishing, Summerlea was to emerge as a grand old lady in a different guise – a residential home for the elderly.

Initially, Summerlea was spoken about in the same hushed tones as the workhouse had once been. It carried a social stigma. It was seen as a place to which elderly residents of the town, no longer able to fend for themselves, were sent to spend their final years. A motley collection of spent souls, spared the rigours of the outside world, as the light dimmed on their lives.

Nothing could have been further from the truth. Thanks to the efforts of the dedicated band of care officers responsible for running Summerlea, a thriving, happy community had sprung up there.

It was now full to capacity – some thirty residents and there was a waiting list – of elderly folk who had discovered a new lease of life.

The driving force behind the spirit of Summerlea was Mrs Gwenda Greatbanks, who firmly believed that while elderly people had their special needs, the way to keep them contented and feel they were still very much part of the world was not to divorce them from the rest of society.

And as the majority of the residents were no longer able to go into Greybridge – certainly not unattended – then every effort should be made and every opportunity taken to bring Greybridge to the residents. So open days, craft fairs, fetes, became the order of the day at Summerlea, which not only helped keep the elderly residents in touch with the younger townsfolk of Greybridge, but also helped to raise much needed funds for little extra comforts.

My first introduction to Summerlea came in the height of summer – a summer that was worthy of the name.

The Summerlea summer fete was being held on the Saturday, with the usual attractions – craft stall, cake stall, tombola, good as new stall, bran tub, various games and sideshows – even pony rides and a little miniature steam train would be on hand for the children,

Mrs Gwenda Greatbanks had phoned the editor to give him advance warning of the event.

The editor had thoughtfully put her through to me.

I tried to sound politely interested.

I must have succeeded.

Mrs Greatbanks couldn't wait to meet me. It was so refreshing to find someone with such an enthusiasm for what she was trying to achieve at Summerlea. She would be delighted if I would consider myself her personal guest on the great day.

I was about as excited at the prospect as being condemned to spend the weekend in wet socks.

*   *   *   *

I was pleasantly surprised. The residents, by and large, were a lively, enthusiastic bunch, each standing guard over their allotted piece of God's earth as they cajoled visitors into trying their hand at one attraction or another, or buying a piece of handcraft, or a cake or two to take home for tea.

Mrs Greatbanks proudly took me under her wing as soon as I arrived, and promptly left me to my own devices some two minutes later, a mother hen responsible for a very large brood.

I was quickly taken in hand by a frail, white-haired old lady who used a walking frame, not so much to aid her mobility, but to help clear a way through the numbers of visitors who had come to support the event.

Her name, I was soon to discover, was Florence Bradshaw, and she had been a resident at the home for some eighteen months, since shortly after her husband died.

She admitted that the thought of being put into Summerlea for the rest of her natural life was depressing for the first few weeks, but gradually, like so many of the residents, not only had she come to terms with the fact that this was now her home, but she was actually enjoying the place.

When we had visited all the attractions that the fete had to offer, I suggested I might buy Florence a cup of tea by way of a thank you for her pleasant company.

She steered me to an area by the side of the old house, where six card tables had been erected and an assortment of chairs set out around them.

"Do you take sugar and milk?" she asked as she powered her way towards the tea stall, frame held at action stations.

"You come and sit down," I said. "I'll get these."

She did a smart about turn.

"If you insist," she said without argument.

I stood behind two ladies who were waiting to be served.

"Two teas, both with. And two rock cakes, Doris," trilled Florence, as she sat down at one of the vacant card tables.

"Coming dear," called Doris, without looking up.

She deftly hauled the spout of the big tea pot over a line of waiting cups and slopped tea into two of them.

"Are those mine?" inquired the first lady in the queue timidly.

"You're next," said Doris, through lips tightly drawn back as the concentration on the task in hand showed in her face.

"Florence is an official."

The lady nodded understanding. She should have known better than to ask.

"Right dear," called Doris.

I moved to the front of the queue.

"I'll take them. How much?"

"Up to you dear."

I fumbled in my pocket and pulled out a handful of assorted coins. I dropped a couple in the soup dish that already contained a collection of silver.

I looked for a sign of approval from Doris. I didn't get it.

I fed the soup dish again.

Still no sign of approval from Doris.

I put the rest of my change into the coffers. Doris's lips drew back in a broad smile.

"Thank you," she said. "Most generous."

"Thank you," I replied. "It's a good idea to leave the donations up to the individuals."

"Exactly what we thought," she said.

"My idea, you know." And without a pause she turned to the lady who had been waiting patiently behind me.

"Two teas coming up."

I took the teas and rock cakes back to the table. Florence had her teeth sank into one of them before the plate touched the table.

*   *   *   *

As I talked to Florence, I began to realise the changes she must have seen over her eight decades.

Summerlea, and all that it had stood for on the day that Florence was born into a working class family in a Lancashire textile town, was a world apart from the family life that she had known as a youngster.

The youngest of eight children, she had lived in a mill cottage for the first twenty years of her life, clothed in hand-me-downs from her elder sisters, eventually following them into the cotton mill that cast its dark shadow over the end of their street on the outskirts of Bolton.

She had been working as a weaver for over six years, when she met Ernest, a driver for the same firm.

They had started walking out together, became engaged and finally married, despite opposition from Florence's father, who had been looking to Florence to look after him in his old age.

In the event, he never lived to see it.

A combination of a lifetime's cotton dust in his lungs, aided no doubt by sixty cigarettes a day since he was twelve, brought his life to a premature end before he was sixty.

And while Florence and Ernest had not had life easy, they had managed to earn a crust, buy their own modest home, bring up three children and share a life filled with its share of happiness for nearly half a century.

She had many tales to tell of the way the women weavers learned to lip read, as they couldn't make themselves heard above the ceaseless clattering of the looms. Of working twelve hour shifts with barely time to breathe in between. Of being awakened at half past five in the morning by the knocker-up tapping on the bedroom window with a long pole.

She recalled with compassion her anxieties as Ernest went off to battle in the first world war, and her ecstasy when he returned. Of the struggle to bring up three young children on her own, all her efforts fuelled by one driving force - hope. Hope of a better standard of living, a peaceful world in which to live, more satisfying work, fairer wages. And hope that one day they would find, in their terms, a modest crock of gold at the end of the rainbow.

It was not to be. But like so many of her generation, Florence had been grateful for small mercies, and had made the most of what she had all through her life.

She was obviously enjoying talking to me almost as much as I was enjoying listening.

But I had to get away. I was trying to think of the best way of making my excuses and leaving, when she beat me to it.

"Well I've enjoyed talking to you," she said at last.

"But I've got plenty to do if you haven't. I must make sure that everything is running smoothly. Gwenda relies on me, you know. Thanks for the tea and cakes."

"Perhaps we'll meet again sometime."

"I hope so," I said. "I really do…"

And with a quick little smile, her dark eyes shining like highly-polished buttons set in her drawn, pale face, she turned and disappeared in the direction of the tombola.

*   *   *   *

Walter Piggin was taking a very keen interest in the structure of a half-eaten chocolate biscuit as I rapped on his door frame the following Monday morning.

He quickly dropped the biscuit into the half-open drawer in front of him and pushed it closed, as I walked into the office without waiting for an invitation.

"Problem?" he inquired, his head cocked to one side.

"Not that I know of," I replied.

He smiled and sat back in his chair.

Or rather, he tried to.

In his haste to close the drawer on his half-eaten chocolate biscuit, he had trapped his tie in it.

As unobtrusively as he could, he shifted the drawer open an inch, released the offending tie, and then sat back.

"So what can I do for you?"

"This fete at Summerlea on Saturday afternoon," I ventured.

"Couple of pictures and captions," rattled Walter.

"No room for anything else."

"Yes. I know about that," I said. "But I got talking to someone while I was there…"

"Don't you mean she got talking to you," muttered Walter, his eyes fixed on the drawer in front of him, and his mind obviously more on his half-eaten biscuit than on my half-baked ideas.

"That's the way it usually is with Gwenda Greatbanks."

"It wasn't her," I replied. "It was Florence Bradshaw. One of the residents."

W.C. waited for me to go on.

"If you could let me have half a page for a feature next week…"

Walter sat upright in his chair.

"Half a page?" he said in astonishment.

He couldn't have looked more staggered if a masked man with a shotgun had appeared behind me.

"She's one of the most fascinating women I have talked to in a long time," I said. "She remembered her whole life with such clarity. Drew such graphic pictures. It would make a great feature."

"If it takes half a page to say it you can forget it," interrupted the editor.

I moved closer to the desk.

"We could run a regular little feature."

He pushed the drawer fully closed.

"There are thirty residents in Summerlea," I said. "Each with a story to tell. An authentic tale of the changes that have taken place during the 20th century and how they've affected their lives. It will make great reading."

Walter considered this for a minute.

"I'll give you a column," he said at last. "As a one off. See how it goes. But I'm telling you, now, I don't think it's going to cause so much as a raised eyebrow."

"It's what's happening today that people are interested in. What affects them. Not the ramblings of a geriatric old maid."

"Well I would hardly call Florence Bradshaw that," I said.

"We'll see," he said.

He swivelled his chair through a hundred and eighty degrees to face the window. The issue was closed as far as he was concerned.

There were far more important things occupying the mind of the editor of the *Pioneer Group of Weekly Newspapers* at that moment in time. Like the half-eaten chocolate biscuit in his desk drawer.

*   *   *   *

I hoped there would be a positive response to my piece based on Florence Bradshaw's memories, if only to prove me right.

I had no idea it would be quite as overwhelming as it turned out to be. There were phone calls and letters from people who recalled similar memories of years gone by. Passers-by were stopping Walter in the street to tell him how much they enjoyed reading about the old days. I knew I had succeeded when I was called into his office on the Saturday morning.

Until this time, he had been reluctant even to discuss the Florence Bradshaw story.

"Won't keep you," he said. "Just thought you'd like to know we have had some reaction from that piece you did on your old maid from Summerlea."

"Good, I hope," I said, trying to sound casual.

"Mmm, suppose so," said the editor. "Good enough to make it worthwhile doing on a regular basis, anyway. Say once a fortnight. I take it you can keep it going for a few weeks?"

"I've no doubt there will be others who come to light."

"All right, all right," muttered the editor impatiently, "Don't get carried away."

"You're very fortunate to have an editor who can spot a good idea when he sees it."

"It was my idea," I started to protest.

"I know whose idea it was, laddie," he said, stroking his moustache with his forefinger.

The series continued to be a great success, and my fortnightly visits to Summerlea became something of an occasion. Always there would be a cup of tea waiting for me, and a welcoming committee consisting of Gwenda Greatbanks, Florence, and, after a couple of weeks, another resident.

She had only just moved into Summerlea, and she stood out from the rest of the residents like a beacon in a snow drift.

She wasn't stooping and bent, grey haired, pale or frail.

She was well-built, with jet black hair, and a rosy complexion accentuated by skillfully applied make-up.

She had bravely fought against the ravages of arthritis for years, but at last she was beginning to lose the battle to lead a normal life. Nevertheless it was difficult to imagine that she was seventy eight, certainly from her outward appearance.

Her name, I soon discovered, was Madge Fenwick, and she made sure that no one forgot it.

She quickly became the life and soul of the party, organising bingo sessions, games of dominoes, encouraging her fellow residents to recite a little party piece as they sat together in the late afternoon, or leading them in a medley of old songs, as she vamped away at the aging piano.

She'd worked as a cleaner, housekeeper, shop assistant, played the piano in a cinema, but it was obvious that the jewel in her chequered life was when she appeared on the stage for over twelve years as one half of a comedy magic act, Hey Presto and Madge.

"Played every theatre in the country," she said with pride

"Played before Royalty twice. Met the Prince of Wales, I did. The old one, you understand."

I nodded.

"It wasn't easy mind, I can tell you. Hours and hours on Crewe station on Sunday afternoons, as you made your way from one end of the country to the other with your props trunk, and your costumes. Making for some grotty little back street digs, where you were fed barely enough to keep body and soul together."

She smiled again, as the fond memories came flooding back.

"But I wouldn't have changed it for the world," she grinned.

"If I could have done that forever, I would have died a happy woman."

"But when he went…" Her eyes misted over.

"Well that was the end of it, wasn't it?" She looked thoughtful as she recalled the sad chapter in her life.

"We were more than a team. We were a part of each other's lives."

"When you're as close as that, well some things you never get over."

I agreed, and quickly moved on to more cheerful days. I'd no wish to prolong the woman's obvious agony by pushing her to re-live those days when she had lost her man and a major part of her life.

It didn't take her long to get back to her usual ebullient self.

There was no holding down her natural bubbling enthusiasm for life for very long.

As I walked back to my car, I could hear the first chords of "The Bells are Ringing" from the upright piano in the lounge as Madge heralded her arrival to lead her fellow residents in another sing-along.

I couldn't imagine anything in the world getting Madge Fenwick down for long.

But I was wrong.

The editor decided that after a dozen or so of my features on times past, it may be a good idea to give it a rest and pick it up again in several weeks time.

I readily agreed.

While it had been my idea in the first place, and I had enjoyed talking to the old folk and writing my fortnightly column, the novelty had tarnished considerable, and I was ready for a break from it myself.

So I didn't have cause to go to Summerlea for some weeks.

Gwenda Greatbanks kept me in touch with events there over the phone, and I promised to drop in whenever I could for a cup of tea and a chat.

But it was some weeks before I got round to actually doing anything about it.

And when I did eventually make it, I was in for quite a surprise.

There were various activities going on as the residents sat in the lounges reading papers, knitting, working on handcrafts, or just sleeping.

But there was no babble of chatter, no laughter. Just silence.

I joined Gwenda in her office.

"Everyone well?" I asked brightly.

"As well as can be expected," replied Gwenda in a matter of fact way.

She went on to tell me of a couple of residents who had been taken off to hospital since I was last there, and other comings and goings.

"And how's my old mate, Florence," I inquired.

"She's not feeling so good today," replied Gwenda. "It's her chest you know."

"I'm sorry to hear it," I said.

"And how about Madge? You have still got her here?"

I could usually hear her booming voice as soon as I arrived at Summerlea.

Gwenda sighed.

"Yes, we've still got Madge. Now there *is* a problem."

"A problem? Madge?"

"Don't tell me they can't stand the pace?"

Gwenda shook her head.

"She's hardly spoken two words to anyone for over a month."

"She hasn't touched the piano. Won't join in any of the games. Spends a lot of time on her own."

"What brought this on?" I was genuinely surprised.

Madge was the last person in the world to withdraw into her shell.

Gwenda shrugged.

"I don't know. All I do know is that it coincided with a new arrival. Mr Clyde. Archie. He keeps himself to himself. He's pleasant enough. But ever since he arrived... well, I don't think he and Madge have exchanged more than a good morning."

"That doesn't sound like Madge," I said. "Perhaps if I had a word."

"You're more than welcome to try," replied Gwenda.

"But I don't think you'll have much luck."

Madge was sitting by the window in the corner of the big lounge when I found her. She was thumbing impatiently through a women's magazine. Her face lit up momentarily as she saw me. Then the smile faded.

Her complexion, without the carefully applied make-up she always used to wear, was paler than I'd ever seen it.

Her garish red lipstick, so hastily put on, gave her face a lop-sided, unfamiliar look. And her hair looked as if it had not been properly combed for some days.

"How are things?" I asked conversationally.

She shrugged.

"Same as ever," she replied.

"That's not what I've heard."

She shrugged again.

"You've been very quiet lately."

Madge looked at me.

"It's a free country, isn't it?"

I realised I was wasting my time. As I looked down into those pale blue eyes, I could almost see the shutters slamming down against me. Whatever was bothering Madge, she was determined to keep it a closely-guarded secret.

As I left to drive back to the office, Summerlea had a very gaunt, cold appearance, it's grime-covered Derbyshire stone shell standing out against the pale sky.

The building was the same as it had always been.

It was inside that the dramatic transformation had taken place.

It was no longer a welcoming haven of warmth and comfort.

It was a dwelling without a soul.

And it all seemed down to one shining light being dimmed.

Whatever Madge Fenwick's problem, there didn't seem to be a person on earth she could or was prepared to share it with.

But life went on at Summerlea, as Gwenda Greatbanks slowly managed to instil some enthusiasm back into her residents once again, as they launched themselves on the new round of fund-raising events.

I didn't have cause to go up to the big house myself for some months. It was usually sufficient to send Martin up to get a picture of whatever they were doing, and to pick up a little caption story by phone, which Dawn usually did.

Then one day, the phone rang on my desk.

It was Gwenda Greatbanks, in a state of some excitement.

"Do you think you could come up to Summerlea this afternoon," she said.

"We're having a little celebration."

"Somebody's birthday?" I inquired.

Gwenda had never bothered to make a special point of it before.

"Much more exciting than that," she trilled.

"An engagement party!"

"Engagement party?"

"That's right."

"Anyone I know?"

"You'll have to wait and see, won't you?" she said impishly.

"See you later."

And she was gone.

I couldn't help smiling.

It was the first engagement party I had ever been invited to in the middle of the afternoon, which would be all over by tea time, and where the guests would get nothing stronger to drink than half a glass of British Empire sherry.

I had to call in at the council offices on the way out to Summerlea, and when I got to the big house, Martin had already arrived.

As I was going in through the front door he was on his way out at the speed of a tom cat on heat.

"Where you off?" I inquired.

"Can't stop," he muttered "Got your picture. I've got to get something on the wire to the nationals."

"The nationals? Hang on a minute…"

But Martin slammed the door of his car and fired the engine. With a screech of gravel he shot off down the drive, past the sign that proclaimed a ten miles per hour speed limit and impatiently joined the stream of traffic on the main road.

Gwenda greeted me inside the front door.

"We've been waiting for you," she said in a mildly scolding voice.

"The couple won't cut the cake until you're here."

"But who…" I pleaded.

"Come along," interrupted Gwenda. And she led the way into the lounge. By the card table, the centre piece of which was a sponge layer cake, topped with cream, was Madge Fenwick, her face wreathed in smiles, her make-up as carefully applied as when I first set eyes on her.

She got up as soon as she saw me.

"About time, too." she said, that old twinkle back in her eyes.

"Now we can get the party going."

"You!" I said in surprise.

She gave me a big wink.

"Who else has got what it takes to get a feller to pop the question in here," she smiled wickedly.

"But who?"

Madge turned to the rest of the assembled throng, stuck two fingers in her mouth and let out an ear-splitting whistle.

The chatter stopped.

"Well come on," she called. "My friend here wants to meet my intended."

From the assembled throng stepped Archie Clyde.

Before I could congratulate them both, Gwenda interrupted by rapping the back of a spoon sharply on the table.

"Well if everyone is here, I think we can start."

"Now we all know why we're here. We're here to celebrate the engagement of two of our dear friends and fellow residents, Madge and Archie. And as far as I know, it's the first time anything like this has happened here since the Summerlea Residential Home was opened."

"So if we can get the happy couple together for long enough, we'll start by cutting the cake. Then we can all join them in a little drink to wish them every happiness in the future, which, of course will be here with us."

Archie Clyde. I still couldn't believe it. The man who had had such a devastating effect on Madge when he arrived. The man she had hardly exchanged two words with when I last saw her. The man responsible for her withdrawing so fully into her shell.

With a glass of British Empire sherry in one hand and a generous slice of jam sponge – made specially for the occasion by Mrs Merryweather – in the other, I finally got Madge and Archie alone.

"I just don't understand," I said to Madge.

"I thought you two couldn't stand each other."

Archie shuffled uncomfortably.

Madge smiled.

"I never did get round to introducing you, did I? This is Archie…"

"Yes, I know," I said.

Madge smiled at me again, her pale blue eyes as clear and sparkling as fresh spring water.

"Better known as Hey Presto."

It took a second or two for this to sink in.

"You mean, you and him…"

Madge nodded.

"That's right. Worked together for twelve years. Married for ten. Until he cleared off with one of the dancers in Rotherham. And I hadn't seen him from that day to the day he walked in here."

"And that's why you changed so suddenly?"

Madge nodded.

"Well you must admit, it was a bit of a shock." She slipped her hand into his.

"But there's been a lot of water under the bridge since Rotherham."

"So you're planning to get married again?"

Archie smiled.

"I don't know whether we'll get as far as that. One step at a time, eh?"

Madge nodded in agreement.

"And I got the impression you didn't even like him," I said.

"Like him?" she said. "What's that got to do with anything?"

Archie put his arm round Madge and drew her to him.

"But she loves me," he said.

"And I love her."

"Right enough," said Madge. "Always have done and always will." She sipped her sherry.

"Can you think of a better reason for wanting to stick together for the rest of our lives?"

12

MRS Eva Murphy was a lady of letters. She lived in Moss Bank, a neat, three-bedroomed thatched cottage set back just off the London Road, about two miles south of Greybridge Pike. It had once been known as the home of Mr Benjamin Murphy, former Mayor of Greybridge, former chairman of just about every male-orientated organisation in the town you cared to name, and purveyor of Murphy's Gold Medal pies, which had been a household name in the town for nearly half a century.

For many years, Eva had lived dutifully in the shadow of her highly-respected husband as he had gone about his business. The one regret of this Polish-born lady was that she had never had any children.

She had very little by way of close family at all.

Benjamin Murphy had a brother who lived somewhere near Cambridge, and a sister who had married well in Scotland, neither of whom Eva had clapped eyes on since her wedding. Her own family were all still in Poland. So with the sudden passing of Benjamin, who was found collapsed one morning on his bakery floor by one of his young assistants, Eva was to all intent and purpose, alone in the world. At least, she would have been had she not been the type of woman she was.

Eva Murphy was never one for the limelight.

She was happy to stay in the background, totally supportive to Benjamin, always content to be two steps behind him. Not for her the constant rounds of meetings, outings, speaking engagements, except, of course, during his year of office as Mayor, when she couldn't avoid it.

Not that she didn't have plenty of opportunity. She did. But whatever spare time Eva Murphy had after seeing to her husband's needs and the day-to-day business of running a home that anyone would have been proud of, was precious to her.

It allowed her to follow her own special interest and all-consuming passion in life – writing letters.

It all began when she started to write home to relatives in Poland, and found that not only did she enjoy it, but actually had a talent for making tasks as mundane as queueing for a lamb chop sound interesting.

After the passing of Benjamin, Eva found even more consolation from her letter writing.

Although she hadn't seen her own family for many years, she felt very close to them through her correspondence, and in turn, she looked forward to hearing from them. She began to think about all the other lonely people there must be in the country. People who would love to correspond with someone, to share their troubles, their joys, or just to share their snippets of news. If only they knew someone who was sufficiently like-minded to want to do the same.

She wrote to the local papers offering to reply to any letters sent to her by lonely people, old or young, who just wanted someone to be in contact with.

Her letter was spotted by an eagle-eyed local radio reporter, who interviewed Eva about her interest in letter writing, and this in turn was broadcast on national ratio.

Soon the whole thing snowballed, and it became almost a full-time occupation for her, replying to all the correspondence she had become involved in.

And she loved every minute of it, happily paying the mounting postage bill out of the sizeable income she received from the estate left to her by her dear departed husband.

She wasn't an agony aunt, as such, although she was the first to admit that she did get her share of other people's troubles dropping through her letter box each morning.

No one actually asked her to do anything but to read what they had written, and reply when she got a chance. It seemed to ease the burdens of so many people just to write down their problems and share them with someone else.

And when that person was someone they didn't know, and they were never likely to meet, it seemed to make it that much easier.

Over the years, Eva Murphy had developed a vast and deep understanding of the human race. And a deep affection for her adopted country and its inhabitants.

She shared her little cottage with two cats – mother and daughter – and just about anyone who cared to drop by and pass the time of day with her.

And always in the corner of her neat living room, to the left of its huge, warm, natural stone fireplace, her bureau was piled high with correspondence from the four corners of the British Isles, awaiting her attention.

She had even had a wooden fixture made in which she could pigeon-hole letters that called for a reply on a certain day.

"To someone on their own, it's something to look forward to," she would say.

"If you know that every Thursday morning, or every other Thursday morning, there will be a letter for you, it can be a real highlight in your life."

"Especially if you have nothing else to look forward to."

"And there are plenty of folk in that situation, believe me."

The last thing Mrs Murphy would ever consider doing would be to betray a confidence, or to disclose the contents of any of the letters written to her.

Nevertheless, she did seem to have a remarkable knack of coming up with quite a few snippets of local chat – as opposed to gossip – which was meat and drink to the *Pioneer*.

When Mrs Murphy called to say she had something of interest for us, we never questioned it. Her years of handling people and their problems at all levels of life, her deep compassion for others, had made her an astute judge of human character.

If Mrs Murphy had come up with a snippet of chat that was of interest to her, we could guarantee it would be of interest to the rest of our readers.

Someone would get out to Moss Bank to have a chat with her as soon as possible.

And there was another reason why Mrs Murphy's calls demanded immediate attention.

She made the best fruit scones in Greybridge.

* * * *

I was returning from lunch at the Mitre shortly after two o'clock one Friday afternoon, when Christine cornered me as I was about to go upstairs to the office.

"All right for some, isn't it?" she called, without taking her eyes off her finger nails, which she was rasping with a worn emery board.

"Thought you were on another half day," she said, still without looking up.

This only meant one thing. She'd had to take a phone call for me, as there was no one else in the office.

"Who was it?" I inquired wearily. It was the fag end of the week.

"Mrs Murphy," she replied.

"Mrs Murphy?" I brightened immediately.

A cup of tea and a fruit scone could be just the tonic I needed.

Either that or an all-expenses paid week in Barbados. And I was realistic enough to know which one I stood the better chance of getting.

"Thanks, Christine," I said, turning back to the stairs.

"She said be sure and take a photographer," she called after me.

"A photographer?"

"That's what she said." She held out her hand in front of her to inspect her nails.

If I was hoping to be enlightened further by Christine, I was out of luck.

* * * *

As I opened the gate of Moss Bank cottage, Mrs Murphy was stooping over a rose bush, secateurs in one hand, basket in the other.

She snipped away at the roses completely oblivious to the arrival of Martin and myself, until Martin let the gate spring shut with a crash.

Mrs Murphy turned, startled.

"Oh, it's you dear," she said, breathing a sigh of relief.

She looked Martin up and down.

"This is Martin," I said. "From the office."

Mrs Murphy smiled. She obviously approved.

"So you work at the *Pioneer* as well, do you?"

"He's our photographer," I explained.

"One of them," corrected Martin.

"Photographer," said Mrs Murphy with some admiration.

"How interesting. I often wish I'd taken up something like that when I was younger."

"I would have thought you had quite enough to keep you out of mischief," I told her.

She smiled that warm smile that started in her eyes and lit up her entire face.

"I expect you're right."

"Well I suppose you'd like a cup of tea while you're here."

"I wouldn't say no," I said.

She led the way into her neat little cottage.

Her writing bureau, as usual, was piled high with letters.

The elder of her two Persian cats was curled up on the big armchair by the fire.

"Make yourselves comfortable," called Mrs Murphy as she headed towards the kitchen.

"I'll just put these roses in water if you don't mind."

"Not at all," I called back.

"What does she want?" hissed Martin impatiently.

"She'll get round to it in her own good time," I said.

"There's no rushing Eva."

The tea and home-made scones went down a treat, as always. It was when we had finished our second cup of tea that I was given a sharp reminder that Martin had another job to go to if I didn't. And still Mrs Murphy had made no mention of why she had called us out to see her.

I tried to lead her into it, without being too direct. I didn't want her to feel that now we had enjoyed her hospitality, we couldn't wait to be off.

"Er, had any interesting letters this week then, Mrs Murphy?" I inquired.

"They're all interesting to me," she said with a warm smile.

"Sometimes I wonder what I've taken on." She indicated the bureau with a broad sweep of her pudgy little hand.

"Who'll answer all those when I've gone?" she asked. "That's what's bothering me."

"You won't have time to go anywhere," I joked. "Not with all that lot to answer. You're far too valuable down here."

She smiled. "I like to think I do my bit to bring a little happiness into people's lives," she said, still with a trace of an east European accent that had a charm all of its own.

We sat in silence for some time.

Our summons was obviously not connected with the letters.

"I knew there was something I wanted to show you," she said at last. Martin quickly got to his feet.

"My patchwork blanket."

"Patchwork blanket?"

He looked at me, raised his eyes to the heavens, and sat down heavily.

"You've finished it then?" I asked politely, trying to sound interested. "Not quite," replied Mrs Murphy. "But I've done a lot more than when you were here last. I'll just go and get it."

"There's no need…"

"No trouble. No trouble at all," she called as she disappeared up the stairs.

"What's a flaming patchwork blanket got to do with anything?" hissed Martin, who by now was getting more than a bit agitated.

"I don't know," I said. "But we'll have to take a look at it now, won't we. We can't just walk out."

"Look at the time," he moaned. "If I miss this one, my dad'll kill me."

"Worth a bob or two, is it?" I grinned.

"And the rest."

Mrs Murphy came back, a huge blanket slung over her arm, made up entirely of knitted squares joined together.

"You take that end," she said, and she pushed one end of the blanket into my hands and stood back.

"What do you think of that?"

"It's... it's very nice," I said. "I would have thought it was finished myself."

"Very nearly," she said proudly. "Perhaps another dozen squares."

Martin gaped at it open-mouthed.

"What are you going to do with it when it's finished?" he asked.

"I'm not sure exactly where it will end up," beamed Eva with pride. "But it could make the difference between life and death to someone."

"Yeah. Like me if I don't get to my next job," moaned Martin under his breath.

He got to his feet.

"Look, Mrs Murphy. This is very interesting, but I do have to get off now."

Mrs Murphy smiled at him.

"Of course," she said. "I understand. Well I do hope you enjoyed your tea and scones."

He glanced quickly in my direction.

"Er, yes. I did. But that's not really what I came for. I came to take a photograph."

"Really?" Mrs Murphy's face lit up again. "Well I am flattered."

"And what would you like to take a photograph of? My garden perhaps? If you'd have let me know, I could have straightened it up a bit."

"Not your garden, Mrs Murphy."

Mrs Murphy looked round the living room. Her face lit up again as her gaze fell on her big blue Persian cat.

"You wouldn't want a photograph of Naomi, would you?"

She indicated the cat asleep on the chair.

"I know she's a beautiful creature, but she's not championship class, I'm afraid."

Martin glared at me.

"I'll be in the car," he rasped. "She'll have me as dotty as her if I stop here much longer."

And he picked up his box and stormed out.

"Have I said something to upset your friend?" Mrs Murphy asked innocently.

I shook my head.

"No. Of course not. He was just wondering, well so was I actually, well what are we doing here?"

She looked at me as if I had two heads.

"You don't know what you're doing here?"

"Well, yes. I know what we're doing here. We came because you left a message…"

"*I* left a message?" she interrupted in some surprise.

"With Christine. At the office," I continued. "While we were out at lunch."

Mrs Murphy shook her head.

"I didn't leave any message," she said.

"I haven't used the telephone all day."

"I thought you and your friend just happened to be passing and had stopped to pass the time of day."

"Er, no," I smiled. "It wasn't quite like like that."

"I do hope I haven't wasted your time," sighed Mrs Murphy apologetically.

"I really thought you had just come to have a cup of tea with me."

"It's never a waste of time having a cup of tea with you, Mrs Murphy." I smiled.

And I meant it.

*　　*　　*　　*

I mounted the stairs to what was the norm on Friday afternoons – an empty office.

Within five minutes, the phone rang.

I picked it up to find myself on the receiving end of a mouthful of abuse that would have shrivelled an icicle from a lady whose cut glass accent suggested she should know better. A lot better.

When she had calmed down, I began to get the gist of her message.

"It really is most unsatisfactory. I spoke to your girl at lunchtime."

"Christine?"

"I don't know what her name is, but she obviously has difficulty understanding plain English."

"I've been waiting nearly an hour, and not one of your staff has been near the place."

"I'm sorry," I said. "I've only just come in myself."

"There appears to be some sort of misunderstanding."

"Misunderstanding!" she shrieked down the phone.

"It may be a misunderstanding to you. But its more than that to me, I can assure you. It's most embarrassing."

"I've all my friends round here from the committee to give me moral support. I've had my hair done specially for the occasion. Really, I would have thought I'd have warranted a little more importance in your scheme of things than to be merely the subject of a misunderstanding."

"Could I ask what the occasion is?" I asked hesitantly.

There was silence from the other end. I could sense her coming to the boil.

"I've only been nominated lady captain-elect of Greybridge Park Golf Club," she bellowed.

"I see," I said, understanding dawning at last.

"I'm sorry. I don't think I caught the name."

"Mrs Murphy," shrieked the caller. "Mrs Violet Murphy. Stoneways, Greybridge Park Road."

"I'll be with you in about twenty minutes," I assured her.

"It's the best I can do, I'm afraid."

She put the phone down before I could bid her good afternoon.

I got in my car and headed out towards Greybridge Park Road, a dual carriageway that led out to the west of the town.

It was a well-kept, tree-lined road of individually designed detached houses set well back from the thoroughfare to allow enough room to show off to perfection the carefully manicured lawns and over-pampered gardens.

I had never met Mrs Violet Murphy. She was one of Dawn's contacts.

But I knew that when I did, the lady captain-elect of Greybridge Park Golf Club would be surrounded by her friends in a setting worthy of a Hollywood movie.

Yet I couldn't help reflecting that it was Mrs Eva Murphy who had the riches beyond compare!

13

ERNIE Padstow was a slightly-built man, who had lived a contented, but in the main, undistinguished, life in and around Greybridge for as long as most folk could remember.

His bent figure, making him look considerably older than his fifty or so years, was a familiar sight, pushing the pedals of his old Post Office bike as he went about his daily business of delivering mail to the south of the town, where the man-made harshness of industry gave way to the softer, natural landscape of the foothills around Grey Tor.

Ernie lived quietly with his wife, Brenda, in a terraced cottage just off the main road.

Fern Cottage was one of a block of six, and at some time or other in their chequered history, each cottage had been home to a member of the Padstow family - Ernie's grandfather, his father, brother, cousins.

Now there was just Ernie and Brenda, no family of their own to carry on the tradition.

Their social life wasn't anything special. Ernie generally spent one night a week at the Post Office Club, and another couple of nights at the British Legion club.

He played a fair game of darts, and the odd game of skittles, but his performances at either game were never noteworthy enough to get him into reckoning for any of the teams.

Brenda, on the evenings she wasn't too tired when she got home from the International Stores where she worked, took great comfort from the various activities offered by St Peter's Ladies Fellowship, and the local branch of the W.I.

In fact, Ernie and Brenda were a fairly average couple, with one notable exception.

When it came to growing gooseberries, Ernie Padstow was head and shoulders above the rest.

A giant among men.

*   *   *   *

The highlight of the horticultural calendar for some miles around was the Greybridge Show.

It had started life over one hundred years ago as the Goose Fair, when

it was a high day in the calendar on which farmers could get together and strike up a bargain or two over a handshake and a pint.

In more recent years, as fruit and vegetables became an integral part of the fair, it had become known as the Gooseberry Fair, not particularly because gooseberries featured any more prominently than any other fruits, but according to local lore, it was a hybrid of Goose and Berry Fair.

Nevertheless, gooseberries were one category each year that brought grown men almost to blows in the quest for honours.

Over the years, the appeal of the fair had widened to include sections for flowers, cage and aviary, fur and feather – even a dog show. But there was no doubt that the real interest in the show was in the fruit and vegetable sections, where men could become overnight folk heroes or reduced to tears on the turn of a judge's decision.

And there was no doubt that the jewel in the crown was the magnificent Alderman Vincent Lane Perpetual Silver Challenge Trophy in the gooseberry section.

There was a fine tradition for growing gooseberries in the town going back well beyond living memory.

And ample evidence that one family had dominated the scene more than any other over the preceding five decades – the Padstows.

It had all started with Aaron Padstow, who was the first man in living memory to carry off the trophy on six consecutive occasions. He was followed by his son Granville, then his son, Albert, who had in turn passed on the secrets of previous generations to the present guardian of the good name of Padstow, young Ernest.

Preparation started early, of course, with none of the principal contestants admitting to any interest in even showing, let alone being in with a chance of winning.

Conversation in the Plough and Flail, where many middle-aged men who spent more loving care tending their allotments than tending to the needs of their own families, used to meet, became fitful and stunted, as initial probes were launched to test out the weight of the opposition.

"Suppose you'll be entering the fair this year?"

"What, after winter we've had? No chance."

"Aye. Think I'll give it a break myself this year."

"Be hard pushed to find enough to make up a decent exhibit."

But it soon became apparent that this was but talk.

Soon the tentative inquiries gave way to talk of mulching and pruning, of thinning out.

Theories as to why one grower had done better or worse over the years than a neighbour working exactly the same ground flowed thick and fast. It was all attributed to using the same knife as his grandfather did for pruning, to the shape of the trench, the distance apart the bushes were planted. Or to some secret ingredient used to feed the eager roots in the final days before the luscious berries reached perfection.

The only one who kept well away from conversation of this kind was Ernie Padstow.

If someone did venture to bring up the subject, he would quickly turn it to talk of the weather, the exploits of the local cricket team, or the proposed new by-pass.

For whatever Ernie's secret, no doubt passed on to him by his forebears, he was determined to take it to the grave, having no sons of his own to carry on the tradition.

Each year, he found as the growing season got underway and the date for the fair approached, he became a very popular man.

His wayward game of skittles overnight became good enough to have him named as travelling reserve with the team. He had even been known to actually play against weaker opposition. Attempts would be made to co-opt him to the Legion entertainments committee, the darts selection panel - anything that would bring Ernie out for a relaxing evening and keep him around later than most, in the hope that someone may be able to loosen his tongue and get him to reveal some hint as to his success when it came to growing gooseberries.

But no one had yet succeeded.

As the big day approached, the conversation became peppered with unfamiliar names to the uninitiated – Leveller, Lancashire Lad, London, Lancer, Whinham's Industry, Ringer – with talk, of potash deficiency, droop and mildew.

The only money being put on with Chester Guthrie, who always ran an unofficial book on the show's various winners was who would come second to the man who had carried off the premier trophy for the past eight years, Ernie Padstow.

This year was going to be no different to any other.

*　*　*　*

One of the hazards of showing prized fruit and vegetables, and winning year in and year out, is that not all your fellow competitors take kindly to it.

And it wasn't entirely unknown for an entire crop to suddenly wilt two days before the show.

Precautions had to be taken.

The more serious contestants were even known to mount an overnight watch to make sure no intruders ventured in the direction of their champion produce.

Ernie was as aware of the dangers of leaving his crop unattended as the next man.

So for the last few days before the show, he made sure that either himself or Brenda was in at the cottage, to keep an eye on the neat little walled garden at the back. A garden surrounded by a high, crumbling brick wall, and secured at night with an equally high sturdy wooden gate that was locked and bolted.

And he had a most effective night time alarm system.

Mickey, the Jack Russell belonging to Mrs Trilby next door, had ears like a hawk and a bark that could penetrate armoured steel. If someone dropped a paper cup on the other side of Grey Tor, Mickey would probably have heard it.

With less than a week to go to the big day, everything in Ernest's garden was rosy as he went about his business, tightlipped, answering casual inquiries about his chances this year with only a non-committal nod or a grunt. But the slight smile that tugged at the corner of his thin lips spoke volumes about what he was thinking.

That night, he carefully locked up, secured the gate to the garden and went to bed with Brenda.

He slept undisturbed until three o'clock in the morning, when the peace of his unconsciousness was shattered, not by Mickey raising the roof next door, but the whimpers of someone in pain.

Brenda was lying beside him, sweating profusely and writhing in agony, holding her stomach.

The other residents of the little block of terraced cottages didn't get much more sleep that night, either.

It was about half an hour later when Mickey shattered the peace with his high-pitched yapping, aroused by the hasty arrival of Dr Manners' car. And he didn't settle down again until nearly an hour later.

Not until the ambulance was well on its way to Greybridge General, carrying Brenda Padstow on her way for an emergency operation for appendicitis.

*   *   *   *

Whilst Ernie Padstow was undoubtedly king when it came to gooseberry growing, while he had never had one complaint during almost thirty years of delivering her majesty's mail, and was in all the ways that

mattered, an ideal husband, when it came to looking after himself, he was a non-starter.

So it wasn't exactly a surprise to learn that Brenda had quickly arranged for her mother to move into Fern Cottage to see that Ernie didn't starve himself to death.

As Ernie related these developments in his domestic life over half of bitter in the Plough and Flail, he seemed rather more cheerful at the prospect than I would have expected him to be at the thought of having his mother-in-law inflicted on him for a few days.

But desperate situations need desperate measures, and Ernest was canny enough to realise this.

"I was upset about Brenda, naturally," he said.

"But it couldn't have come at a worse time."

"Not with but a few days to go to the show."

"I mean I'm sorry she's laid up and that, but life must go on. And I wasn't fancying the idea of leaving my fruit unguarded at this stage."

"What are you planning to do then? Sit her out there all night with a loaded shotgun?" I asked, half in jest, though nothing would have surprised me.

"No need for that," smiled Ernie. "Just so long as there's somebody around during the day, while I'm out on my rounds."

"And she does turn her hand to a fair steak and kidney pie," he reflected.

I didn't see Ernie again until the following evening, when I called in to

126

ask him how things were going, and to see if he'd object to our getting a picture of him beside his prize gooseberry bushes before he stripped them of the pick of their produce for the show.

He was in an affable mood. Full of good humour and steak and kidney pie.

"No problem," he said. "At least it'll show one or two folk around here that I grow them myself. Which is more than I can say for some of 'em."

I tried to get him to enlighten me, but he refused to say any more. His mother-in-law came in from the back.

"I thought I'd go shopping in the morning," said Mrs Grimshaw, casually. "So if there's anything special you want…"

She got no further. Ernie quickly stopped her, a flash of alarm in his eyes.

"Do you think you could leave it till after dinner?" he appealed.

Mrs Grimshaw looked surprised. "Why?"

"Er… well I'll be home then. There'll be someone in the house," muttered Ernie quickly.

"Are you expecting visitors?"

Ernie didn't want to go into a long explanation about the desirability of having someone around to keep an eye on his precious gooseberries. He very much doubted that Brenda's mother would view the fruit bushes with quite the same reverence that he did, and his sanity had been in question on numerous occasions through his apparent preoccupation with his garden.

"Not especially," murmured Ernie. "It's just that, well in case the hospital wants to get in touch," he said in a rush, as what he thought was an excellent reason came into his head.

"And why should they do that?" asked Mrs Grimshaw. "Brenda's perfectly all right. It's just a matter of time."

"I just thought…" Ernie began to reply. Why did the woman have to be so awkward? But he was cut short.

"Still if it means that much to you, it doesn't matter to me whether I go in the morning or the afternoon."

Ernie breathed a sigh of relief.

Now that little problem was out of the way, he could turn his mind to more serious matters.

Like uncorking a bottle of his home-made elderberry wine.

*   *   *   *

I arranged to take Martin along to do the picture on the following day – the day before the show.

We arrived at Fern Cottage just after two o'clock. Ernie was usually back by one.

The front door was slightly open. I knocked.

No reply.

We went inside.

I called Ernie's name.

Still no reply.

I went through to the kitchen.

The door to the neat garden at the rear of the cottage, it's fruit trees standing dutifully to attention like a well-drilled guard of honour, was open.

Squatting on the ground next to his beloved gooseberry bushes, head in hands, was Ernie.

"Ernie," I called as I went to join him.

He didn't look up.

"Are you all right?"

He thrust a piece of notepaper into my hand.

I read it quickly.

It seemed that Brenda's younger sister, Jenny, who lived in Stoke on Trent and was expecting a baby, had gone into premature labour, and her husband was away on a business trip until the evening.

Brenda's mum had got the first available bus, with a promise to be back in time for supper.

"So what's the problem?" I asked, the weight of the catastrophe still not dawning.

Ernie looked up at me with heavy eyes.

"They must have been watching the place," he choked, with a lump in his throat.

"The bastards must have been watching her every move."

He indicated his gooseberry bushes.

For the first time, the awful truth hit me.

There was hardly a gooseberry to be seen.

The bushes had been practically stripped of every gorgeous, luscious berry!

* * * *

That evening, I called in at the Plough and Flail.

The sole topic of conversation was Ernie Padstow's shock withdrawal from the show. The field was now wide open.

"Haven't you any idea who might have done it?" I asked Ken the landlord.

128

"Not one of my regulars, that's for sure," he grunted.

"It might be their life's ambition to get their hands on that cup."

"But none of 'em would stoop to this."

I believed him.

"It must have been someone from out of town."

"All I can think of."

"But I'm telling you, if we hear one whisper about who it is, we'll chop his flamin' hands off."

There was an approving grunt from anyone in earshot.

There was a lot of sympathy for Ernie.

Not that that was much comfort to him right now.

As I drove back to Fern Cottage, I felt sick inside.

Ernie was slow to answer the door.

I followed him inside, asking if he'd got any idea at all who might have done this thing to him.

He shook his head silently.

"I've had a word in the Plough and Flail," I told him.

"I'd swear it was none of those lads. They're as mad about it as you are. They all wanted to see you beaten. They'll admit that. But not this way."

He sat down heavily, gazing at the remaining gooseberries from his prize bushes in a bowl in front of him.

"They don't look half bad to me," I volunteered, "Maybe you could get enough out of that lot for an exhibit."

He shook his head.

"Not in the same league as my show fruit."

I waited for him to go on.

"Well that's me finished."

"Four generations of Padstows have been taking prizes at that fair for as long as I can remember."

"Four generations. And it has to end like this."

"There's always next year," I said.

He shook his head.

"If it's come to this. If this is the only way they can stop me..." he looked at me with sad, heavy eyes.

"I don't bloody well want to know."

He got up and went to the kitchen.

I heard the sound of gushing water as he filled the kettle.

There was a tap on the front door.

Ernie made no move to answer it.

The tap was repeated, more urgently this time.

"I'll get it," I volunteered.

I opened the door to Mrs Grimshaw, rosy-cheeked with the exertion of her walk from the bus stop.

"Where's Ernest?" she asked, looking round.

"In the back."

"I'm sorry I'm late. I had to hang on till Terry got back."

"Anyway, he's back now and he's promised to ring me as soon as anything…"

Ernie emerged from the kitchen.

"Now did you get some tea?" gushed Brenda's mum.

Ernie shook his head.

"See what happens when there's nobody here to fetch and carry for him?"

"Our Brenda was right. He'd have been a shadow by the time she come back."

She turned her attention back to Ernie.

"Give me ten minutes. There's a shepherd's pie in the fridge. It only wants warming up."

She moved to the hall door.

"And I've got a lovely gooseberry pie for after."

Ernie looked at her in disbelief.

"I made a couple while I was at it. And I took some over to our Jenny. She was delighted."

"Only it seemed such a waste."

"All them lovely gooseberries out there."

"I knew you'd no intention of doing anything with them."

"Not with our Brenda in hospital. And by the time she came out…"

She was interrupted by the piercing squeal of the kettle.

If Ernie heard it, he certainly showed no outward sign.

He sank slowly into a chair by the table, his knuckles white as he clenched his fists tightly together, his face approaching the colour of one of his prized gooseberries.

His mother-in-law headed for the hall.

"Well come on. Surely it's not beyond you to brew the tea while I take my coat off."

"Not after the day I've had!"

14

THE Meadows seered along the shallow river basin into the heart of Greybridge like an intrusive green gash in the industrial landscape. Preserved for all time as a place for the enjoyment of the public under a deed of covenant going back centuries, with certain rights bestowed on needy citizens for the grazing of their stock, it had been the industrial equivalent of the village green for as long as folk could remember.

This was where high days and holidays had been celebrated through the ages, the activities changing with the passing years, but the spirit remaining as strong as ever.

This was where the children came sledging and sliding, slithering and skiing as the cold fingers of winter held the town in its icy grip.

Where the first crocus and snowdrop raised their hopeful heads to the world, closely followed by one of the finest shows of daffodils for miles around.

During the summer, it played host to the visiting fair on Whit Monday and August Bank Holiday.

Throughout the year, the khaki and green tents of the Scouts and Guides were in evidence, as young people worked to win their badges in woodcraft, cookery, pathfinding, orienteering and a dozen other interests that appealed to the inquiring minds of youth as they strove to develop into responsible citizens in a confused world.

On the nearest Saturday to Midsummer day, there was a host of outdoor sporting activities as artisans and professional folk from the town took up arms of combat to keep alive yet another ancient tradition in the town, which was reputed to go back to the sixteenth century.

In those days, life itself could be the prize of victory for the combatants.

Today, the activities were more gentle, though none the less keenly fought. Welly throwing, tug-of-war across the river, raft racing, log chopping.

And for the hardy – or extremely foolhardy, depending on your point of view – New Year's day brought the opportunity to purge away the evils of the past year and start all over again by jumping from what remained of the old stone pack horse bridge, which according to many historians had been instrumental in giving the town its name, into the gently-flowing, chilling waters of the stream below.

The Meadows was all things to all people in Greybridge, and there were few people whose lives the rambling, meandering strip of pasture and woodland had not touched.

Indeed there were more than a few who probably owed their very existence to the inviting warm privacy of the thick foliage that abounded in the sweet-scented pine woods on a pleasant summer's evening.

*   *   *   *

Dolly Paxton was as much a part of Greybridge heritage as the Meadows themselves.

Now she was retired, she spent endless hours walking the myriad of paths, accompanied always by her ageing Shetland sheepdog, Pepper, and clutching a well worn Marks and Spencer carrier bag, in which she would collect a berry here, and a leaf there, which she would take home to dry out and transform into brightly coloured Christmas decorations, set in pine log bases – her contribution to the sale of work to raise funds for the church roof, or some other urgent requirement necessary to keep Christianity warm and dry during the chill winters.

There was hardly a man, woman or child in Greybridge who didn't know Miss Paxton. She was an imposing figure, whose close cropped hair and horn rimmed glasses would have given her a masculine appearance were it not for her ample bosom.

She had worked most of her life in Greybridge Central Library, where her knowledge of the books was almost legendary. When Miss Paxton was on duty, there was never any need to consult the index. She could tell you whatever you needed to know in an instant.

She lived alone in Toll Gate House, not more than a stone's throw away from where the path led down from the main road towards the Meadows, and which suggested that at one time, the incumbent had the right to make a lucrative living charging travellers a modest fee for entering the town. This right had long since disappeared, of course. But not the mystery surrounding Miss Paxton's personal life. Stories abounded as to why there were no men in her life.

It appeared she was an only child, and the favourite theory for her present situation of spinsterhood was that she had devotedly looked after first her ailing mother, then her ailing father until at last they had passed away, by which time Miss Paxton was too old and too set in her ways to consider marriage.

There was another tale that she had had but one love in her life - a young man who worked for the town Highways Department, who went off to serve his country at the outbreak of war, promising to return to her, to make their two lives one and live happily ever after. But he was reported missing in action, and from that day to this, Dolly, deep down, had always held out the hope that he hadn't perished, but would one day turn up again.

Whatever the reason, she was a singularly lone person, though not lonely. It was purely out of choice.

And while she was happy to pass the time of day with anyone, at the first hint of the conversation becoming over-friendly or probing, she would be on her way.

Reclusive, private, a bit of an odd character by most standards, Miss Paxton may have been.

But there was no doubt that she was very much a part of the very fabric of Greybridge.

*   *   *   *

It was nearly ten o'clock before Elliot Forbes phoned in. He wouldn't be in the office today. He was still in bed and thought it advisable to stay there. He seemed to have picked up some bug or other that was doing it's best to blow the top of his head off.

No, it was nothing to do with the eight pints of bitter, lord knows how many whiskies and the odd vodka and tonic he must have consumed at the Parks Superintendent's retirement party the previous night.

But, out of consideration for his fellow workers, he had decided to stay off to spare us the risk of catching it too.

So it was nearly half past ten when I arrived at the police station to do what should have been Elliot's call to get the list of crimes perpetrated in Greybridge during the previous twenty four hours. The *Herald* reporter had been and gone.

Sergeant Jim Blacker was on the desk, and he was having a rough time. He was trying to take down details of a missing dog, being reported by a wizened little man without a tooth in his head and enough lines on his face to pass off as an Ordnance Survey map of the Peak District.

"Be with you in a minute," Jim called, as I walked in.

I nodded.

Jim turned his attention back to the old man,

"Well we'd better have a few details," said Jim wearily.

"You will find him?" pleaded the old man. "He's my only companion you see. Since the old lady died."

"We'll do our best," replied Jim wearily. "Now the sooner we get a few details down, the sooner we can get cracking."

"All right?"

The old man nodded.

"Name?"

"Ben."

The old man's lips quivered as he said the word.

Jim started to write.

"Surname?"

"Westover," said the old man dutifully.

"Same as mine."

Jim stopped writing.

"Same as yours?"

"That's right. I'm Jack Westover. My dog's Ben Westover."

"I didn't want the dog's name. I wanted yours," said Jim impatiently.

"Right. Let's start again."

"*Your* name."

It took some five minutes for Jim to get down the information he wanted.

It seemed that Ben was a ten-year-old border collie.

Old Jack had been out shopping with him and had tied him to a drainpipe outside Woolworths in Commercial Road. When he had come out, Ben had gone.

I didn't know whether I felt more sorry for Jack, who was obviously upset by his loss, or Jim, who would have found it easier to extract bee's teeth than get the information he required from the old man.

At last, they were finished. Jim said they would keep an eye open and if they heard anything they'd be in touch with Jack.

Jack's eyes misted over. "*If* you hear anything?"

Jim hastily corrected himself.

"*When* we hear anything."

Jack smiled his thanks.

At that moment, the police station door opened and the face of a young lad, perhaps ten years old, peered round. Apparently satisfied by what he saw, he ventured in.

"Yes, sonny," inquired Jim. "What can we do for you?"

"Has anybody lost a dog?" muttered the lad.

"Black and white. Getting on a bit."

Jack's ears pricked up.

"Have you seen it?"

"Tied up outside," said the lad casually.

"You lost one, mister?"

Jack didn't reply. He was out of the door with a speed that belied his years. He let out a little squeal of delight.

"Ben, you old rascal."

Jim looked down at the lad.

"Seems like you've made an old man very happy," he smiled.

Jack came back through the door trailing a piece of washing line behind him, on the end of which was the black and white border collie.

"It's him," he called. "It's my Ben."

He turned to the lad.

"I don't know how to thank you. Where did you find him?"

The lad was non-committal.

"Wandering about. He could have got run over if I hadn't grabbed him. You're very lucky to have him back."

"I know, I know," said Jack rubbing Ben's ears fondly, as the dog sat obediently at his feet.

"Was there a reward then?" asked the lad, without any signs of emotion.

"Reward?" Jack had clearly never even considered the thought.

"Well, yes… I suppose there is. Er, how much?"

He looked at Jim.

Jim shrugged.

"It's up to you. Pound…"

The lad looked horrified.

"Pound! I've walked all this way for a pound? I wish I'd never bothered now."

"Now listen here sonny," I could see the anger rising in Jim at the boy's mercenary attitude.

But Jack cut in.

"I'll give you two," he said.

"I know he's worth more than that…"

He looked down at Ben, who had his soft brown eyes trained on Jack's face.

"But it's all I can afford."

"It'll do, I suppose," said the lad without an ounce of gratitude. Jack took a worn leather purse from his pocket and opened it up, just as Andy Lane came out from the back and into the office.

Andy had not been at Greybridge police station much above a month, and I hadn't seen much of him.

He wasn't the sporty type, wasn't Andy.

He recognised the lad immediately.

"Hello Terry. What you doing here?"

Young Terry looked decidedly sheepish.

"Just called in," he mumbled.

Jack took the two pounds from his purse.

"Not found any *more* stray dogs, have you?"

Terry looked even more uncomfortable.

"Wandering on the main road," he muttered.

He snatched at the money in Jack's hand.

"Thanks, grandad. See you."

"Hang on a minute," Jim called.

Terry headed for the door, obviously with no intention of stopping. He never reached it. He ran straight into my arms.

"What's all this about stray dogs then?" Jim asked.

Terry was silent.

Jim turned to Andy for an explanation.

"I was down at Bridgefoot Terrace, Sarge. Couple of days ago. Car break-in."

Terry looked away.

"Seems Mrs Massey's dog had run off, and Terry here had found it."

136

"Did he now?" asked Jim, eyeing Terry, who was paying close attention to his scuffed shoes.

"I don't suppose there was a reward?"

Andy nodded.

"She give him a couple of quid, right Terry?"

The lad turned away without answering.

Andy was as baffled as I was.

"What's it about, Sarge?"

Jim nodded in the direction of Ben who had now flopped down and was lying quietly at Jack Westover's feet.

"Lad here just brought him in. Said he found him wandering down Commercial Road."

He turned his attention back to Jack.

"He hasn't got a collar on has he, Mr Westover?"

"Never had a collar," replied Jack. "Never needed one."

"He never goes away from home, see. Except when he comes to town."

"Then I never let him out of my sight."

"Well, not as a rule."

"That's why young smart ass here couldn't take him straight to your home," said Jim.

He turned his attention to young Terry again.

"And how many more have you pulled?"

Terry didn't reply.

"Right lad. I think we'd better have a word with you in private."

"Andy..."

"Right, Sarge."

Andy moved to the public side of the counter.

"Come on, lad," he said. "This way."

Terry decided there was no point in arguing. He meekly moved towards the door being held open by Andy.

"Just a minute," Jim interrupted.

"Haven't you forgotten something?"

Terry turned.

"What?"

"You know." Jim held out his hand.

Terry pulled the two pounds from his pocket and pushed it into Jim's hand.

With a last glance at Jack and Ben, he headed for the interview room.

Jim handed the money to Jack.

"This is yours," he said.

"And if you take my advice, you'll use it to buy Ben a collar and a disc

137

with his name and address on. You don't know how lucky you are to see him again."

Jack was still bewildered by the events that had taken place.

"But the lad brought him back. He deserves something."

"The lad took him in the first place," explained Jim.

"And you're right. He does deserve something."

"And if his parents have got anything about them, he'll get it. Now off you go. And don't forget that collar."

"I won't, sir. I won't," gushed a grateful Jack.

"Come on boy." Ben dutifully got to his feet and followed Jack out, as I held the door open.

"Sorry about that," grunted Jim wearily.

He picked up the mug of coffee that had been standing by his elbow for at least twenty minutes.

He took a sip, pulled a face and put it down again.

"It's been one of those flaming mornings," he said.

The Inspector hasn't even put in an appearance yet. Talk about sergeant flaming dog's body. Stick a brush up my behind and I'll sweep up an' all."

"Parks Superintendent's retirement do last night. Inspector was there, I take it?"

Jim nodded.

"Doubt if you'll see him this side of lunch time," I said.

"There seems to be some bug going about."

"Elliott's got the same thing."

"He reckons its a case of flu."

"More like a case of scotch!"

Jim wasn't amused.

"That's all I need, isn't it? I don't know why I stick it, honest I don't."

"Of course you do. It's a way of life."

"It's not my way any more, I can tell you. It used to be fun being a copper. It wasn't easy, I'm not saying that. But we had a few laughs along the way. Now everything's so flaming depressing. You wouldn't believe half the things that folk get up to these days."

"I'll get the book."

He went to get the incident book. I had to admit he was looking weary.

As he turned back, the phone rang.

"Here we go again," he muttered, as he put the book down and went to answer it.

"Greybridge police station. Yes, Miss Paxton…"

He pulled a notebook towards him, glancing across at me and raising his eyebrows.

It was obvious that this call wasn't going to do anything to improve Jim Blacker's humour.

Suddenly, he looked interested.

"I see," he said. "And when was this?"

"Right. Well we'd better have a full description."

"Well as full as you're able…"

He picked up a pen.

"Well how about clothing for a start. Was it dark, light?"

He started to write.

"That's fine. Anything else? Shoes?"

"I see…"

"Right, now was he a big man?"

"Well, above average?"

"You'd say he was well-built. Yes, that's very handy. Now can you remember anything else? Well, hair for instance. Colour, long, short… that kind of thing."

Jim turned his attention to his notebook again.

"Gingerish. Curly… Long? Short?"

"Average length. Right. That's fine."

"Now anything else you can tell me?"

He paused as he waited for Miss Paxton's reply. It was obviously not very helpful.

"Well was he clean-shaven?"

"He *wasn't?* Right. Yes. That's a big help. Well can you tell me what colour his beard was?"

Jim Blacker glanced up at me, and turned away so I couldn't see his face.

"Right Miss Paxton. I understand. We'll send someone round to see you as soon as possible. In the meantime, you've been very helpful."

"Goodbye, now."

He replaced the phone, desperately trying to stifle his laughter.

"I'm sorry about that," he said at last.

"Indecent exposure on the Meadows. Miss Paxton was walking her dog."

"I shouldn't think she found it very funny," I replied.

"It isn't," sniggered Jim. "It was Miss Paxton. Her description."

"I heard it," I said.

"Well-built, short, curly, ginger hair, unshaven. I didn't hear what she said about his clothes."

"You didn't hear what she said when I asked her about his beard," smiled Jim.

"She said she never saw his face!"

"Funny," I grinned.

"I could have sworn somebody said it was no fun being a copper any more."

15

HARRY Renshaw and his wife of twenty years, Peggy, were just about as big a contrast as nature could make them. Peggy was a round, jolly woman, large of build and large of personality. She must have weighed in at nearer twenty stone than ten, her body festooned in friendly chubbiness, giving out a warmth that everyone who came into contact with her was instantly aware of.

Her round, rosy-cheeked face, set with a small, soft mouth, a podgy little nose and hazel eyes that shone like jewels from her weather-beaten skin, broke into a thousand creases whenever she smiled, which was long and often.

Harry, on the other hand, stood a little over five feet in height and weighed in at no more than seven stone, wet through.

His skin was pale, his hands hardened through years of manual work at Fogden's bakery, and his features were sharp to match his wit, and increasingly frequently, his temper.

On the occasions that Harry and Peggy had been seen out together, their joint appearance had been cruelly likened to a sideways view of a penny farthing bicycle.

But the occasions on which they did venture out together were few and far between.

Garden Cottage was a solid tribute to the weathering properties of Derbyshire stone, the date 1745 engraved above the front door. It boasted some five acres, much of which was let out for grazing, and the rest Peggy worked as a supplement to Harry's meagre earnings.

Her apples, pears and plums were legend in the late summer and autumn, but much of her income came from poultry. She sold eggs and provided the odd roasting chicken for much of the year, and before Christmas she would bring on a hundred or so turkeys to grace the festive tables in the area.

Her work kept her busy from early in the morning until well into the evening – an arrangement that did not lend itself to a very active social life, as Harry worked the night shift at Fogden's, starting eight o'clock in the evening and often working through until eight the following morning.

For many couples, this sort of arrangement would have spelled marital disaster, but in the case of Harry and Peggy, was probably responsible for them having a marriage that worked so well.

I was introduced to the Renshaws shortly after I arrived in Greybridge through Dawn. As well as collecting her weekly dozen free range eggs from Peggy each Monday morning, she was kept well informed of what was going on in her neck of the woods by this jovial lady who seemed to pass the time of day with half the population of the town during the course of a week, and knew just about everybody's business.

It wasn't because she was nosey. She was a sympathetic person who had that most precious gift of having the time and the interest to listen to other people's problems and seeing them on their way, if not totally unburdened, at least happier in the knowledge that they had shared their troubles with someone.

Not that Mrs Renshaw was a gossip. She wasn't. She was a caring person, who used to impart snippets of information to Dawn only if she thought some practical good would come out of them.

There were many who considered her to be overbearing, accusing her of being the type of person who insists on helping old ladies across the road, even when they don't want to go.

But her heart was in the right place, and if there is any truth in the adage that you only get out of life what you put into it, Peggy Renshaw must surely have been in line to scoop the jackpot.

It was, in the main, her public spiritedness that led to so much conflict with Harry, who felt that he should be number one in his wife's considerations at all times. And should he ever have been in need of Peggy's ministrations, there was no doubt that he would have been. The truth was that there were many folk worse off than Harry Renshaw.

And Peggy seemed to attract them like flies to a jam pot.

*   *   *   *

Individually, Harry and Peggy were great people to know.

Peggy for her caring, cheerful approach to everything and everybody, and Harry for his humour.

For what he lacked in inches and muscle power, he had been adequately compensated with a razor sharp wit that had done much to lighten many a Saturday or Sunday lunchtime in the tap room of the Greybridge Arms.

After my first introduction to Peggy, I became a regular visitor to Garden Cottage, collecting a dozen eggs most Thursday mornings. At this time of day, Harry was usually fast asleep in bed, but I never had to ask. I could tell as soon as I went into the outhouse where Peggy sorted the eggs.

If she greeted me with a cheery wave, her face lighting up into a smile as bright as a beacon, I knew her husband was tucked up warm and comfy, alone with his dreams.

If she merely went about her business, politely passing the time of day but no more, I knew that Harry had some other business that had kept him from his slumbers and was still very much awake and around the house.

Similarly, if there was no reply from the outhouse, and I went to the cottage, I could tell as soon as Harry opened the door whether Peggy was on the scene. He, too, would be making a supreme effort to keep the peace, wary of saying anything that could be taken to be in the slightest contentious.

But if she wasn't there, he twinkled with good humour, a star in search of a galaxy in which to shine.

Until one Thursday morning in early October, when the bottom dropped out of Harry Renshaw's world.

*   *   *   *

The town hall clock was striking eleven as I drove into the cobbled yard at the back of Garden Cottage.

I knocked sharply on the outhouse door as I strode cheerfully in.

"Morning, Mrs R," I called.

There was no reply.

The eggs were in two huge wicker baskets, as usual.

The white paper bags in which they were sold were piled neatly on the disused dairy table that served as counter. Next to them, was the rusting biscuit tin that served as a makeshift till. It was empty.

The outhouse was empty.

I went outside and walked round to the chicken runs.

"Mrs R?"

No reply.

I walked round to the back door of the cottage. The top half of the stable door was open.

I rapped on it.

Still no reply.

"Mrs R?" I called again as I went through the tiny wash-house into the kitchen.

Seated at the table, gazing into space, was Harry Renshaw.

He looked as if he'd seen a ghost.

"Are you all right, Harry?" I asked.

He turned his eyes towards me without replying.

It must have been two hours at least since he had got home from work.

He still wore the overalls that protected him from the grease and grime of Fogden's maintenance department. His face sported a short, scrappy stubble. His eyes were heavy with tiredness, and encircled with a redness that indicated things were far from all right.

"I was looking for Peggy," I started.

Harry stared straight ahead of him again.

"She's gone."

"Gone?"

"Gone. Buggered off," muttered Harry through clenched teeth.

"I never thought it'd come to this."

"Not in a million years."

"But where? What happened?"

Harry shrugged.

"Had a few words last night."

"Nothing out of the ordinary. Usual thing. You know. Get home this morning. She's gone. Buggered off."

I couldn't believe it.

"What on earth did you say to her?" I inquired.

Harry continued to stare straight ahead.

"We just had words," he said, matter of factly. After all it was a fairly regular occurrence.

"I thought it'd all have blown over by time I got home this morning."

"It allus does, see."

He shook his head, his eyes began to fill up.

"I can't believe it. Not that she'd go this far."

"Not my Peg. Not after all these years."

"Perhaps you've got it wrong," I volunteered, trying to sound hopeful.

He swung round in my direction, his eyes blazing.

"Got it wrong?" he yelled. "Do you think I'm going doo-lally, or what?"

I decided it would be wiser under the circumstances to pass on this one.

"I meant perhaps she hasn't left you," I said at last. "There's probably a perfectly reasonable explanation."

"She's gone all right," he said more calmly.

"She's never been out of the house when I've got home before. Never in all our married years."

"Allus been here to have my breakfast on the table."

"But this morning…"

He put his head down and rubbed his eyes, partly out of fatigue, partly out of disbelief that such a thing could have happened.

"Bed was all made up. Like it had never been slept in."

"Suitcase had gone."

"Best 'un. One we got new to go to Colwyn Bay."

"And there was this note." He pushed across half a sheet of notepaper.

On it were written the words, in Peggy's unmistakable block capitals, "No more milk until further notice".

"She must have gone off in such a tearing hurry she forgot to put it out."

Things were not looking promising.

"Do you know what clothes she's taken with her?" I asked.

"It might give you an idea."

"Clothes?" he interrupted. "How would I know? I don't know what she's got and what she hasn't, do I? I never noticed things like that."

I could well believe it.

Peggy could spend the morning stark naked, and I doubt whether Harry would have noticed, so long as he got his breakfast on the table when he got in.

"Perhaps she's gone to visit a friend," I volunteered.

Harry looked at me as if I was out of my mind.

"Without telling me where? Or why?"

He did have a point.

"Perhaps if you phoned one or two of her friends?" I suggested.

"We haven't got a phone," he grunted.

I was about to point out that there was a call box at the end of the lane, when he grabbed hold of my arm.

"There must be summat you can do," he implored. "You know about these things."

I shrugged.

"I'm sorry, Harry. I don't know what to suggest."

"What about the police?"

"They have detectives."

I tried to explain that she was hardly a missing person. Not yet, anyway. It couldn't have been above a few hours since she had taken her leave.

As far as we knew, she was in no danger, not mentally deranged, nor was there any other reason why the police should become concerned. Not at this stage.

"Don't know what we pay our rates for," he mumbled.

I was about to suggest he might ring the hospital.

Perhaps she had nipped out and met with some kind of accident.

But I thought better of it.

Gloom and despondency were already etched across Harry Renshaw's face. I didn't want to add to his burden at this stage.

"Look, I'll have to get back to the office," I said.

"I'll have a word."

"A word?" he said with suspicion.

"At the police station. Unofficially. See if anyone has seen her recently. And I'll ask Dawn and Gary to keep their eyes open."

"There may just be somebody…"

The panic surged into his eyes.

"I don't want anything in the paper," he said quickly.

"I know your type when you get hold of something like this. Heavens knows what people'll think of me when you've finished."

"It's not that kind of paper," I tried to assure him.

"Look, just leave it with me. Trust me."

He looked at me again. He didn't reply.

He had no alternative.

I told him I'd be in touch later in the day. Or before, if I heard anything.

I might as well have been talking to the wall.

Harry let his head drop into his hands, alone with his thoughts.

* * * *

When I got back to the office, I called Jim Blacker at the police station to see if they had had any reports of an accident. I explained briefly what had happened.

"Serves the old bugger right," muttered Jim.

"I wouldn't have spoken to a dog the way I've heard him speak to that woman."

No doubt there were many who would agree with him, but it did nothing to ease the pain that Harry was going through at that moment.

Jim promised to call me if he did hear anything, but said he wasn't very hopeful.

I rang off. My next call was to Greybridge General. My heart started to pound as the duty sister in casualty went to check the admissions over the past 12 hours.

She could hear my sigh of relief as this line of inquiry, too, drew a blank.

It was nearly half past three before I was able to get away again. I had heard nothing more.

It was with a feeling of emptiness that I drove out of town and headed for Garden Cottage.

I had to admit that Harry's fears seemed to have been realised. Wherever Peggy had gone, she had no intention of letting Harry or anyone else know about it.

* * * *

As I drove round the back of the cottage, I hoped that wherever she had been, Peggy had thought better of it and returned to the fold.

But inside the outhouse, things were exactly as they had been that morning.

I crossed the cobbled yard to the house.

Harry was in the living room, pouring himself a cup of tea. He had washed and shaved, and by the look in his eyes, had managed at least some sleep.

"There's another mug in the kitchen," he muttered without looking up.

I took the mug from the wooden draining board and returned to the living room.

Harry made no move to fill it.

"I'm sorry Harry," I started.

"I know," he said. "Not a word."

"You'd have been in touch, else."

I picked up the teapot and started to pour.

147

"She can't just have disappeared from the face of the earth," I said.

"She must be somewhere. I really think you should try her address book. Phone a few of her friends. I'll give you a hand if you like."

He looked up at me as he turned this over in his mind, picked up his mug and noisily slurped his tea.

"I'm sorry, Harry. I know how painful this must be."

"You know?" he erupted. "YOU know? You know NOTHING!"

"How do you know what it's like to be married to a woman you worshipped for 20 years?"

The surprise must have been apparent in my face.

"Aye, worshipped," he said. "I know we had our differences of opinion, but what married couples don't? Tell me that?"

I had to agree, although when it came to the average marital disagreement, I couldn't think of anyone off hand who was even approaching the same league as Harry and Peggy.

"I'm telling you, if I only had her here now, I'd take back everything I've ever said. I would. That woman was solid gold. And I was too blind to see it. Too full of my own self importance."

There was a snick as the outside door to the wash-house was opened.

Harry stopped in mid-flow.

Peggy came into the living room, amazed to see the pair of us there.

"What are you doing up at this time?" she asked as Harry gaped at her in open-mouthed astonishment.

She turned to me.

"He's harder to shift than fog, you know. If it wasn't for me he'd never get to work at night."

Harry's lips started to move, as he struggled to control himself.

It seemed I was about to witness a moving, passionate reunion.

I was wrong.

"Where the hell do you think you've been, you silly mare?" he bellowed.

"Who do you think you're calling a mare?" protested Peggy.

"Well I'm not talking to myself," growled Harry.

"Do you know what I've been through today? Have you any idea?"

"I've only been to mother's," replied Peggy, still shocked by Harry's outburst.

"With a flamin' suitcase?" bellowed Harry.

"I took her that electric blanket," she yelled back.

"That one that you won't have on. It seemed daft having it stuck in that drawer while nights are as cold as this."

She held up the empty suitcase.

"Can you think of a better way of carrying it?"

"Do you know what I've been through today?" blustered Harry again. "Have you any idea…"

Gone was the remorse of the tender husband who would forfeit his last breath for a glimpse of his devoted wife once again.

This was the old, self-righteous Harry.

The Harry that Peggy had known and loved in spite of everything for more than 20 years.

"I left you a note," she protested, as he paused for breath.

"Note?"

"On the table," explained Peggy, moving towards us.

"What did you think that was?"

She pointed to the half sheet of notepaper.

Harry picked it up.

"And what kind of message is this?" he yelled.

"No more milk till further notice."

Peggy took it from his shaking fingers, looked at it and her face split into a broad grin.

"Oh, dear," she said.

"I wonder what the milkman made of the note I left for him."

"Gone to mother's. Back at tea time!"

16

ARY sat back in his chair, feet on the corner of his desk, and
watched intently as a dozy wasp made slow progress up the inside
of the grimy office window.

He couldn't move quickly or stealthily enough to get into position for
his favourite pastime of bringing his wooden ruler down on the
unsuspecting creature, so he screwed up his bank statement into a tight little
ball and hurled it at the insect.

It was so far off target, the wasp never even flinched on its ponderous
uphill journey.

Gary was bored.

We were fortunate in having him with us at all. He was merely passing
time until he was summoned to the New York office of *Time* magazine to
take up his true vocation in life - that of globe-trotting, in-depth
investigative journalist, uncovering corruption, fighting for the rights of
oppressed peoples the world over. He was wound up like a coiled spring,
ready to leap into action the minute the call came. We knew this for a fact.
He had told us often enough.

In the meantime, his attention was firmly fixed on the wasp.

*   *   *   *

If Gary was honest with himself, he would probably admit that he was
more than happy to be at the *Pioneer*.

It suited him. He was reasonably paid. The hours were flexible. And
the opportunities for putting one over on some unsuspecting person or other
were plentiful enough to tax his scheming brain to the full.

It wasn't as if he hadn't had the offer of other work. He had. More or
less every week, recently. And some of the jobs were real plums.

But it was all part of this game that Gary was involved in. The game of
life.

The *Pioneer* published on Thursday morning, so from mid-morning
Wednesday - for those not involved with the actual printing of the paper -
the pressure was off for a few hours.

It was at this point in the week that Gary came to life. Thursday was his
usual day off, and he liked to make adequate preparation for it.

For more often than not, Thursday was an exciting day for Gary these days. A day that could take him to almost any part of the British Isles. At someone else's expense.

* * * *

Preparations started the previous week, when the *Press Gazette* filtered through to our office from the editor's desk. Gary would waste no time in going through the situations vacant columns, selecting possible targets for next week's outing. It could be a newspaper in Nuneaton, a magazine in Morecambe, or a trade publication in Tenby. It depended entirely where Gary's fancy was to take him.

He would select a job not too far removed from his qualifications - on paper, anyway - post off a copy of a well-written letter of application stating that he would be available for interview next Thursday, together with a CV that glowed so much it dazzled. Then he would sit back and wait. More often than not, he would get a phone call the following day to fix a time.

This gave Gary the opportunity to confirm they would pay for his travel, and he would be all set for another free day out.

On Thursday morning, he would set off for his chosen destination, go for his interview, pick up his expenses - which usually included lunch - then spend the afternoon at his leisure, returning to Greybridge in the evening without having spent a penny of his own money.

All that was needed to bring the flirtation to an end was a phone call the following day to say that he had thought the matter over most carefully, and decided it would be in everyone's interests if he didn't accept the job, always assuming that it was offered to him.

There would be words of regret from the other end of the phone that he felt that way, and frequently, expressions of disappointment, because Gary certainly knew how to sell himself at an interview. And that would be that.

Until next time.

Each week, we expected to hear of Gary's downfall as something went wrong with his little scheme. But it never did.

He had the whole business off to a fine art.

In fact, if Gary were to admit it, he had it made in just about every aspect of his life.

Every aspect, that is, except one.

And that one exception aggravated him like a thorn in the sock.

* * * *

One of the perks of working for a weekly newspaper - or any

newspaper for that matter - was the occasional facility trip, which gave us a short, all-expenses paid break in return for a report of the event or service we had been privileged to be part of.

It was a public relations exercise, pure and simple, and such trips ranged from a free seat on the Greybridge British Legion Club annual coach trip to Blackpool, to an inaugural air flight to some exotic location.

During my first few months, there had been one or two facility trips, which, once the invitations had arrived on the editor's desk, were purely in his gift.

The inaugural flight to Paris by a newly-launched airline never saw the light of day. Walter and his wife snapped up that one.

But the rest of us had shared in the generosity of our benefactors, too. Dawn had been to the Chelsea Flower Show as a guest of the Flower Club. I had enjoyed an unforgettable four days travelling to and from the Dutch bulb fields, courtesy of British Rail. Elliot had taken a week's holiday touring the Yorkshire Dales in a sumptuous, luxury motorised caravan, courtesy of a new dealership.

The only exception was Gary.

And he didn't take too kindly to the situation at all.

But if Walter Piggin was anything, he was fair. And he regarded these facility trips as something of a reward in return for the effort we put in, week in, week out to get the *Pioneer* out on time.

And viewed from that standpoint, Gary was a not exactly in pole position.

The situation erupted when Dawn was handed her second trip of the year. The Townswomen's Guild had decided to charter the Orient Express to take them down to Ascot for Ladies' Day. Through their own sterling efforts, they managed to sell the required tickets, and the *Pioneer* was invited to send along a reporter and photographer to cover the grand occasion.

It was obviously a trip that was tailor-made for Dawn, and Martin had been earmarked to take the pictures. It was Phil's day off anyway. Mysteriously, it was Phil who joined Dawn on Greybridge Central Station to sadly report that Martin had gone down with some bug or other, and he felt he just had to make the sacrifice and give up his day off so the ladies and the paper wouldn't be let down.

The fact that he subsequently made the equivalent of a modest pools win out of colour prints of the ladies in all their finery was completely beside the point!

For the rest of that week, Gary went round with a face like thunder. As soon as the paper arrived on his desk, he turned straight to Dawn's report

and Phil's page of pictures. We waited for his outburst. It never came. He calmly wound a piece of paper into his typewriter and went to work.

*   *   *   *

When the editor came into the office, he had the fruits of Gary's labours in his hand.

Dawn was out on call. Elliot made a hasty exit, as he saw W.C. enter with what he considered to be the makings of an advertising feature. This was usually Gary's cue to make his excuses and leave as well, leaving me to pick up the pieces. But he stood his ground. There was even a trace of a smile on his smug face.

The editor waved the paper in the air.

"Why?" he asked.

Gary's eyes glinted with triumph.

"You don't seem to have a lot of faith in me," he replied.

"So I thought the only way was to show you what I could do."

"It's very good," conceded Walter. He turned to me.

"Dawn's Orient Express trip," he said by way of explanation.

I wasn't a lot wiser.

Gary enlightened me.

"If all we're going to do is treat these facility trips as publicity for the organisers, they're a waste of time, aren't they?"

"And in that case..." he tapped the page that contained Dawn's report.

"It's a complete waste of a once-in-a-lifetime experience."

"I thought she did quite a good job," I said.

Gary tilted his head back slightly, giving him what he supposed was an added air of authority.

"She reported on a train trip to Ascot," he said.

"Any train trip. This was the Orient Express. It's something special."

"An experience that most of our women readers can only dream about."

"We had the chance to bring it home to them. And what do we do? Fill the paper with pictures full of their self-importance in their ridiculous hats."

"When the readers picked this up..." he stabbed again at the offending page. "They should have felt they were *on* the Orient Express."

"Where's the atmosphere? The hand-crafted inlaid rosewood decor reflecting a by-gone age of grandeur? Where's the unforgettable experience of eating cream teas off china plates with solid silver cutlery, while they relaxed in sumptuous armchairs as they were whisked through the English countryside, much of it as unravaged by time as the carriage in which they were travelling?"

He paused for effect. Walter was obviously impressed.

I was astounded. I never realised Gary had it in him.

But then again, on reflection, there was no telling to what heights he could ascend in pursuit of a free trip.

The editor thanked him for the interest he had shown and assured him that as soon as a facility trip came up which would be suitable for Gary's obvious talents, he would be given due consideration.

In the meantime, if only he could bring himself to apply himself to the job in hand with as much enthusiasm as he had to putting his case for a free trip, everyone would benefit.

Walter returned to his own office.

"Why do I bother?" muttered Gary after the departing figure of the editor, as he reached for the *Press Gazette*.

"Why do I flaming well bother."

But his gloom soon lifted. Within an hour, he had his letter of application and his glowing CV tucked up snugly in an envelope ready for posting.

Pisspot Piggin could stick his facility trips.

*   *   *   *

The job he had applied for this time was in the West Country, some 20 miles from Plymouth.

The following Monday morning, the phone rang on Gary's desk. He wasn't surprised - neither were we - to hear that the call was from the West Country newspaper, to invite him down to an interview later in the week.

"Well, Thursday's my day off," Gary told the caller.

He listened. "Morning or afternoon? Well I've been thinking about that. It's a long trip from here. So I thought I might come down on Wednesday afternoon and stay overnight."

There was silence once again.

"I appreciate you don't normally pay overnight accommodation expenses," continued Gary. "But you must admit it is a long way to make the return trip in one day. In fact I wouldn't have even thought of applying if it hadn't been just the job I was looking for. And I'm sure you wouldn't have bothered inviting me down if you weren't interested in me."

He paused again.

"Certainly I'll hang on."

He tapped the desk with the fingers of his free hand, his expression giving no indication of what was going on at the other end of the phone.

Suddenly, his face split into a grin.

"That's fine," he said.

"Ten-thirty it is then. See you on Thursday. Bye."

He replaced the phone.

"I take it you got what you wanted," I said. "As per usual."

"The jackpot," he beamed.

"Return rail fare, overnight hotel, all at their expense."

Gary was on cloud nine.

His euphoria lasted all of 24 hours.

*   *   *   *

When Walter Piggin came into the office the following morning with the mail, he had the hint of a smile on his face and he was making a game attempt to hum "Scotland the Brave".

We had all seen the signs a dozen times before. He was looking for a volunteer to give up a night off, though I was at a loss to figure out what it could be for, I must admit.

It was nowhere near Burns night. As far as I knew there was no Scottish connection with any of the jobs in the diary. Yet all the signs indicated that the editor had something of a celtic nature foremost in his mind.

Gary sank lower into his chair.

Elliot noted he was late for his police call and beat a hasty retreat.

Dawn suddenly remembered an urgent phone call she had to make.

The editor rocked backwards and forwards on his heels and looked round the room.

He turned his attention to me.

"How's the diary looking next weekend?" he asked.

"About average," I replied.

"So we could spare someone?" It was half statement, half question.

Gary turned his back on the editor.

Dawn urged the phone to be answered at the other end.

"Well, yes. I suppose so."

I waited for the pay-off.

"Only we've had this invitation for a member of the editorial staff to go up to Scotland for the weekend. Thursday afternoon until Sunday evening…"

Gary suddenly sat bolt upright.

Dawn hurriedly finished her call.

"Scotland?" I repeated.

"It's not definite yet," replied the editor. "I said I'd ring them back. So if we can spare someone…"

I assured him we could.

The editor nodded his approval, turned and retreated to his office.

Gary was out of his chair and after him quicker than a greyhound out of a trap.

I looked at Dawn and shrugged.

"I don't see how we can stop him this time," I said.

*   *   *   *

Gary sauntered back into the office, returned to his chair and casually sat back, at peace with the world.

"Well?" I asked.

Gary smiled.

"I take it you're going?"

"Who else?" he replied pompously.

"What is it exactly?" asked Dawn.

"He didn't say," smirked Gary. "Why should I bother who's footing the bill. It's a long weekend in Scotland, isn't it? All expenses paid."

"Whereabouts in Scotland?" I inquired.

"Cairngorms," replied Gary. "And with my family background…"

Dawn looked at him in some surprise.

"What family background?"

"Scottish side of my family," said Gary in a matter-of-fact fashion. "Mother's side. Highlands are riddled with them."

This was news to me.

"Since when?" I asked.

"Since he told us about the trip," grinned Gary.

And he turned his attention back to his newspaper.

"Haven't you forgotten one little thing?" Dawn ventured.

Gary looked up.

"Like what?"

Dawn smiled. "Like Plymouth."

Gary dropped the paper as if it had suddenly caught fire.

"Damn." he muttered. "Just my flaming luck."

"If you don't want the Scottish trip…" I offered.

He mouthed something in my direction, picked up the phone and dialled a ten figure number.

"Put me through to the editor," he said, his voice laden with sadness, as the phone was answered at the other end.

*   *   *   *

It was late in the afternoon, after a lengthy lunch at the expense of the local Chamber of Trade, before the editor was able to enlighten Gary further.

He had made a call on his way back from the Greybridge Arms, and was now in possession of the full itinerary for the Scottish weekend.

Gary was ready and waiting, as he had been for most of the day.

"Right, laddie," the editor addressed Gary with an unsteadiness in his voice.

He held out a large brown envelope.

"Itinerary is in there," he announced.

"Together with a list of everything you'll need."

"I'll expect a piece so full of colour, you'll be able to smell the heather."

He tried to smile, but it came out more like a crooked leer.

"You've got it," smiled Gary happily as he took the envelope.

The editor turned to me.

"Have you got a minute?" he asked.

And without waiting for a reply, he turned and headed in the direction of his office.

I got up to follow him.

Gary had eagerly ripped open the envelope and was studying a detailed list that seemed to be on notepaper headed by a crest of some kind.

As his eyes took in the document, he visibly went a couple of shades paler.

*   *   *   *

Walter Charles Piggin was looking down on the bustle of late afternoon Greybridge as I joined him in his office.

I could almost feel the aura of well-being that exuded from him.

"Well?" he asked.

"Well what?" I queried.

"What did he say to that?"

"Who?"

"Our friend Gary."

He smiled.

"I didn't stay to find out," I replied.

"I know he's over the moon…"

"Over a barrel, more like," grinned the editor.

"He leaves the Armoury at two o'clock Thursday. By truck. With the Territorial Volunteer Reserve. They drive up to the Cairngorms and spend the weekend under canvas on a survival course. No rations."

"They eat what they can find or they don't eat at all."

"Still, as long as the lad's happy…"

"Happy?"

"He was the one who plagued the life out of me for a facility trip. Well he's got it."

"And if there's one thing I really strive for here, it's to keep my staff happy."

"Do you know," he said, "there are some days when I feel I must be the happiest man in the world."

He produced a crumpled, gaily-coloured packet from the drawer in front of him.

"And this is one of them."

He thrust the packet in my direction.

"Have a chocolate digestive."